HOW I SURVIVED MIDDLE SCHOOL

I Heard a Rumor

By Nancy Krulik

SCHOLASTIC INC.

New York Toronto London Auckland Sydney
Mexico City New Delhi Hong Kong Buenos Aires

ISBN-13: 978-0-439-02557-7
ISBN-10: 0-439-02557-5

Published by Scholastic Inc.

12 11 10 11 12/0

Printed in the U.S.A. 40
This edition first printing, September 2007
Book design by Jennifer Rinaldi and Alison Klapthor

For Danny B.

Hey! Can You Keep a Secret?

Are you the go-to girl when your friends have a secret to share? Can you be trusted to keep the info under wraps or are you known for your loose lips? Take this quickie quiz and find out where you stand.

1. **You just saw your BFF's boyfriend sharing a slice of pizza (and some secretive smiles) with an attractive stranger. What do you do?**
   A. Call your BFF and tell her right away — after all, she has a right to know!
   B. Confront him and find out what's going on before telling your pal.
   C. Keep quiet. You have no idea what the deal is between these two. Why start trouble?

2. **The meanest mean girl in the whole school is bragging to everyone that she made the honor roll this marking period. But you know it's not true because you saw her last history**

test – with a big fat F on it. How do you handle this hot gossip?

A. Start spreadin' the news! It's about time everyone saw this girl for the liar she really is!
B. Keep it to yourself. You may not like the girl, but that doesn't mean you have to sink to her level.
C. Tell only your very best friends, who dislike her as much as you do.

3. You've got the greatest news! You overheard two teachers talking about your best bud. They say she's the winner of the student council election, but they won't be announcing the results until tomorrow. What's your plan of action?

A. Even though it's gonna kill you, your lips are sealed. It'll be even better for your friend to find out the good news in front of everyone.
B. Grab your cell and hit the speed dial. You've got to tell your friend the news and spare her another sleepless night.
C. Tell all your other friends, so you can plan a surprise victory party for your winning friend.

4. You're at a party and no one seems to notice you. But you have a secret weapon that could make you the center of attention – a juicy piece of gossip about two of the teachers in your school. You saw them together outside of school – holding hands! Do you

A. Whisper the info to a few close friends who you know will be impressed by your inside scoop.

B. Keep it to yourself: Even teachers deserve a little privacy.

C. Make your way into the crowd and fill everyone in on the news. After all, if they wanted to keep the relationship secret, they shouldn't have been out in public.

So, are you the kind of person who lets the skeletons out of the closet? Or is MYOB your motto? Add up your points to see what kind of secret keeper you are.

1. A) 1 B) 2 C) 3
2. A) 1 B) 3 C) 2
3. A) 3 B) 1 C) 2
4. A) 2 B) 3 C) 1

10–12 points: Wow! You are the most super secret keeper of all time. You could be tempted with ice cream or tortured with your dad's oldies, but you'll never tell! Just remember, while it's great to be trustworthy, some secrets shouldn't be kept. If you have a friend who may be in serious trouble, be sure to let a grown-up you trust in on the scoop.

7–9 points: Okay, so once in a while you let the cat out of the bag when you're not supposed to. Hey, you're only human, right? Still, spilling even a small secret can be dangerous. Friends have been lost over less. So if you want to hang on to your pals, keep your lips locked.

4–6 points: Well, one thing's for sure — you're not the person to tell a secret to . . . ever! You just can't keep yourself from gabbing the gossip. But there is a way to keep from spilling the beans. MYOB! You can't blab what you haven't heard, right?

Chapter

ONE

I HATE RAINY DAYS. Especially rainy Mondays. Waiting for the school bus while the bottoms of your pants are getting all wet, your sneakers are becoming soggy, and your umbrella keeps blowing inside out is not the best way to start your week. But that's what was happening to me that Monday morning.

I sighed and added another rule to my growing list of very important things that they never tell you at sixth grade orientation.

MIDDLE SCHOOL RULE # 11:

GET A LIFT TO SCHOOL ON RAINY DAYS OR ELSE YOU'LL SPEND THE DAY WRINGING OUT YOUR JEANS.

To make matters worse, I had to stand at the bus stop with Addie Wilson. Of course, *Addie* wasn't going to have to spend the school day in soggy jeans. She'd been smart enough to wear a skirt and waterproof boots to school. Addie was going to look perfect all day long – as usual.

At the moment, Addie was talking on her cell phone.

Probably to one of the other Pops. That's what my friends and I call Addie and her group of friends – the Pops. As in *popular.*

I think every school has its own crowd of Pops. You can spot them a mile away. They're the ones who wear the coolest clothes, have the best makeup, and only hang out with each other. Basically, they're at the top of the middle school food chain.

"No, I'm serious," I heard Addie say into her phone. She paused for a moment as the person on the other end said something. "Well, I wouldn't tell anyone but you, that's for sure," Addie said. "And we certainly can't tell Claire. You *know* she can't keep a secret."

I giggled quietly. Obviously Addie was revealing a big secret to the person on the other end of the phone.

Addie glanced in my direction, rolled her eyes, and sighed. Then she turned her back to me and began whispering to the person on the other end. "I have to talk quieter," she said. "Jenny McAfee is eavesdropping."

I was about to say that I wasn't eavesdropping, she was just talking loudly. But if I said that, Addie would know that I had been listening to her conversation. And technically, that *was* eavesdropping. So I just kept my mouth shut.

Watching Addie whisper into her cell really upset me. *I* used to be the person Addie told her secrets to – back when we'd been best friends.

But that was then. When we'd been in elementary school. Addie and I were middle-schoolers now. And ever since we'd walked through the doors of Joyce Kilmer Middle School on the first day, Addie had decided that she was too cool to be my friend.

I breathed a sigh of relief as the yellow bus finally turned the corner toward our stop. Any minute now I'd be out of the rain – and away from Addie. My friend Felicia would already be on the bus. And she always saved me a seat.

Now *I* would have someone to talk to, too.

"Over here, Jenny," Felicia called from the back of the bus as I climbed on board.

I smiled and trudged my way toward her. I wrinkled my nose as I sat down. The bus stunk – like a mix of mildew and wet dog fur.

"What a yucky day," I groaned as I sat down on the damp green plastic seat.

"Not if you're a duck," Felicia giggled. She looked down toward my feet. "Boy, your pants are really wet."

"I know," I said. I was wet from the cuffs of my pants all the way up to my calves. "I had to wait a long time for the bus."

"That stinks," Felicia said.

"It sure did," I told her. "Especially because I had to listen to Addie talking on her cell phone the whole time."

"What was she talking about?"

"Who knows?" I shrugged. "Some very important Pop secret, I guess."

"I didn't think their secrets could be important," Felicia said with a shrug.

I had to agree with her. The Pops spent all their time either talking about makeup or saying bad things about everyone else in school. I wasn't particularly interested in either of those kinds of conversations.

So how come I was dying to know what Addie had been whispering about?

That was the Pops' best-kept secret: Somehow they'd figured out how to make everyone in the school hate them *and* want to be one of them, at the exact same time.

By the time my fifth period lunch rolled around, my jeans had dried. Unfortunately they were now stiff as a board, and there was a line of mud along the bottom. They looked awful – but not nearly as bad as my hair. It was a flat, stringy mess. That's what happens to my hair in the rain. It just hangs there like limp spaghetti.

But that's not what happened to Addie's hair. As I glanced across the cafeteria, I could see that her hair still looked great. She'd pulled it back into a tight blond bun. A few of the curls had fallen from the bun and were framing her face. She looked like a model.

Eergh! It was so frustrating.

"I'm singing in the rain . . ." Just then, my friend Chloe

made her presence known by singing and dancing her way across the cafeteria toward our table. "Just singing in the rain. What a glor –"

"Somebody stop her," Marc groaned from across the table, putting his hands over his ears. "She's been singing that same song all day. You should have seen her jumping in puddles at our bus stop."

"That's what the guy did in that old movie," Chloe explained.

"You're not in a movie," Marc reminded her.

"I could be. . . ." Chloe hinted. She pointed to Marc's backpack where he kept his video camera.

"I already told you, *no*," Marc said. "My movie is a spontaneous documentary. No acting allowed."

"So I'll just jump up right now and start dancing spontaneously," Chloe suggested.

"*Spontaneous* means it happens at the spur of the moment," Marc said with a sigh. "It's not spontaneous if you plan it."

Chloe shrugged. "Your loss," she told Marc. Then she laughed and burst into song again. "The sun'll come out tomorrow . . ."

Just then, Addie and her two best friends, Dana and Claire, walked past our table. They were heading for the girls' room. That's where all the Pops hung out after they'd finished eating. None of them ever had to actually go to the bathroom or anything. They just went in there to put on makeup and gossip about people. The girls' room near the cafeteria was sort of like their headquarters.

Dana stuck her fingers in her ears as she walked by. Addie whispered something to Claire, which made her giggle. They may have been whispering, but there was no doubt they were making fun of Chloe.

Chloe wasn't bothered, she just kept right on singing as the Pops walked by. They had a busy schedule to stick to – there were lots of other people to make fun of before lunch was over.

I had to give Chloe props for how she'd reacted to the Pops. Addie, Dana, and Claire's whispers must have hurt her feelings. But she wasn't going to let them know that.

"This rain really stinks, doesn't it?" I said, changing the subject.

"Tell me about it," my friend Carolyn groaned. "No field hockey practice for me after school today."

"Can't you practice inside?" I asked her.

Carolyn shook her head. "The basketball team is practicing in the gym this afternoon."

"That's okay," Carolyn's twin sister, Marilyn, consoled her. She looked around at all of us. "We can hang out at our house after school. Maybe rent a movie or something."

"Not me," Josh said, shaking his head. "We've got a Mathletes competition on Wednesday. I've got practice."

Josh is a mega-genius. He's in sixth grade like me, but he's already taking seventh-grade math.

"Lucky you," Carolyn told Josh. "You can have practice rain or shine."

"Algebra equations are fun for all seasons," Marilyn added with a giggle.

"I can come over," I told the twins. "I barely have any homework so far today."

"Count me out," Marc said, shaking his head. "Film Club is meeting after school."

"Guess that means we can rent a chick flick, " Marilyn said with a shrug. She looked over at me. "Wanna ask Rachel and Felicia to come, too?"

I shook my head. "They've got basketball practice."

"Oh, well," Carolyn said. She glanced over toward Liza, a small, dark-haired seventh-grader who hung out with us. "Are you free?"

"Sure, I can come for a while," Liza said. "But I have to get home pretty early. I have a science quiz tomorrow."

"Cool. Chloe, how about you?" Marilyn wondered.

Chloe took a sip of her juice. "I . . . um . . . today?" she said.

The twins nodded. "When else?"

"I can't today," Chloe said. "I . . . er . . . I have play rehearsal."

"No you don't," Liza corrected her cheerfully. "They're using the auditorium for a teacher meeting after school, remember?" Liza was painting scenery for the play, so she knew the rehearsal schedule as well as any of the actors.

Chloe bit her lip slightly. "Oh, yeah," she said. "I forgot.

But . . . um . . . I still can't do anything with you guys today. I have plans."

"Well, then what are you doing?" Carolyn asked.

"I'll just have to take a rain check," Chloe told her.

Josh glanced over at the cafeteria windows. "Nice choice of words," he joked as he watched the downpour outside.

I glanced over at Liza and the twins curiously. They shrugged. Obviously, they'd noticed it, too.

Chloe sure was acting weird – even for her.

"NO, I'M TELLING YOU, it was really strange," I told Felicia Tuesday morning while we were riding the bus to school.

"What's so weird about Chloe being too busy to hang out after school?" Felicia asked me.

"She was just being so secretive about it, like whatever she was doing after school was some big mystery," I said.

"Yeah, I guess that is kind of weird," Felicia said, nodding her head.

"What could be such a big secret?" I wondered.

"Maybe she has a boyfriend," Felicia suggested. "Someone she doesn't want the rest of us to know about."

I laughed. Felicia was really into that sort of thing. She liked to read books about dating, and romantic comedies were her favorite kind of movies.

"He could be a guy from the play," Felicia continued. "Maybe even a seventh- or eighth-grader."

"I don't know . . ." I began.

But Felicia was on a roll. She had the whole scene set up in her head. "Maybe he's an eighth-grader. Or someone who goes to another school. A mysterious stranger who came into her life . . ."

I started to laugh. Felicia was going a little overboard

now. "On a white horse, right? And his last name is Charming?" I teased her.

Felicia giggled a little. "You know what I mean." She glanced toward the back of the bus, where Addie was sitting all by herself. (There are no other Pops on our bus and Addie would never be caught dead sitting on the bus with a non-Pop.) "Wouldn't Addie just die if Chloe found a boyfriend before she did?"

I shrugged. Somehow I didn't think Addie would care. She never paid attention to anything my friends and I did. "Speaking of Addie, I've got to meet with her after school," I groaned. "We have to figure out the decorations for the post-election party."

"Is it still a luau?" Felicia asked.

I nodded. "A big one. It's not just for the sixth grade anymore, either." I sighed. Originally, the party was supposed to be for just the kids in our grade, as a celebration after our student council elections. But once the kids in the other grades heard Addie Wilson was planning it, they all wanted to join in. Imagine! Eighth-graders wanting to come to a sixth grade party! That was the power of the Pops.

MIDDLE SCHOOL RULE # 12:

ANYTHING THE POPS ARE INVOLVED WITH IS AUTOMATICALLY COOL.

"Is it hard working with Addie?" Felicia asked.

"Not too bad. But sometimes she gets bossy," I admitted.

"That's when you have to remind her that you're class president – and she's the vice president," Felicia said.

That fact still amazed me. I beat Addie Wilson in the sixth grade student council election. Sure, it was only by a few votes, but I'd won just the same.

"I'd rather we just worked as a team," I told Felicia. But we both knew Addie wasn't exactly a team player. Which was why I wasn't really looking forward to meeting with her after school.

As the bus turned into the school parking lot, Felicia and I spotted our friend Rachel waiting for us by the door. We hurried off the bus to meet her.

"Hey guys, happy Tuesday!" Rachel greeted us.

I groaned.

"We're one day closer to the weekend," she reminded me cheerfully.

"True," I agreed with a laugh. "But I wish it was Friday already."

"Speaking of the weekend," Rachel continued, "Do you guys want to go to the mall to get something to wear to the luau? My mom said she'd take us."

"Sounds fun!" Felicia exclaimed. "We should get some flower things to put in our hair."

"And I was thinking maybe a pretty flowered shirt," Rachel said.

She looked over at me. "You want to come with us, Jenny?"

"Sure," I said. "My mom said I could get a new dress or something."

"This party's going to rock," Rachel said. "I heard Addie's hiring a live band."

"What?" I asked, my eyes opening wide with surprise.

"Didn't you know?" Rachel wondered. "I thought Addie was supposed to be running everything past you before she did it."

"She was," I replied. "And we don't have enough money in the budget for a band."

"Looks like you and Addie are going to have a lot more to discuss this afternoon than decorations," Felicia said.

I frowned. This wasn't going to be fun. Not at all.

I watched as Addie and Dana headed toward the soccer field together during gym class later that day. They were walking *thisclose* to each other and whispering. Every now and then they would look over at one of us non-Pops and giggle hysterically.

Annoying much?

I did not want to go near either of them. But I knew that I had to talk to Addie. I would have done it at lunch, but she always sat with a whole table of Pops. It would have taken more guts than I have to walk over there to talk to her. This way, it was only Dana and Addie I had to face.

I hurried to catch up to them. As I came up behind Dana, she stopped and turned around suddenly. "Do you want something?" she asked, sounding annoyed.

"I . . . um . . . I need to talk to Addie," I said.

"Well . . . um . . . here she is," Dana said, imitating the nervous way I was talking.

Addie giggled slightly and then bit her lip to keep herself from laughing any harder. "What do you want?" she asked me.

"I just wanted to ask you about the luau," I said. "We're still doing decorations after school, right?"

Addie nodded.

"Also, I heard a rumor that you're hiring a band for the dance," I continued. "And the problem is, we don't have the money for live music. You were supposed to check with me before you did anything like that, remember?"

Addie bristled slightly at that. She didn't like the idea of having to check in with anyone about anything.

"Well, for starters, it's not definite yet, so there was nothing to talk to you about," Addie barked at me. "And if I do get the band, it won't cost us anything. My friend Jeffrey's older brother, Elliot, is in a *high school* band, and they'd play for free as a favor to me."

Wow. A high school kid was willing to do a favor for Addie. That was seriously impressive.

"Of course, if you don't want a high school band, and you'd rather have Mr. Jenkins play DJ again . . ." Addie let her voice trail off.

I frowned. Mr. Jenkins was a good math teacher, but he was a lousy DJ. "No, the band will be fine," I told her. "I will . . . uh . . . sign off on it after school today." There. That sounded quite presidential.

"Whatever." Addie rolled her eyes.

As I walked away, I could hear Addie and Dana giggling, which hurt my feelings. Of course, that was exactly the point.

"Hey, Chloe, there you are," I said, as I walked into Spanish class later that day. "Listen, Rachel, Felicia, and I are planning on going shopping for clothes for the Luau. You want to come with us?"

"Can't. I'm busy," Chloe said, plopping into the chair beside me.

"I didn't even tell you when we were going yet," I said. "You might be free and –"

"Not possible. I've got things to do every minute that I'm not in school," Chloe said.

"What kinds of things? We'll be going on Saturday, and there are no play rehearsals on the weekend, so . . ."

Chloe shook her head. "I'm busy," she told me firmly.

"What's so important that–" I began. But before I could finish my sentence, Señorita Gonzalez walked into the classroom.

"*Hola, clase,*" she said.

So much for finding out what was going on with Chloe.

* * *

I called Felicia as soon as I got home from working on the decorations with Addie. "Okay, now I'm convinced something's up with Chloe," I told her after I described our conversation in Spanish class.

"And she wouldn't tell you anything about her plans?" Felicia asked me.

"Uh-uh. Not a word. It's so not like her. Usually Chloe gives way *too* much info."

"I know," Felicia said with a laugh. "Like the time she told us that she wears underpants with the days of the week on them."

"On the *wrong* days." I giggled back. "*Definitely* TMI. That's what makes this so weird. Keeping secrets is really unlike Chloe."

"Some romances are meant to be secret," Felicia told me.

"I still don't think it's a romance," I argued. "It could be anything. Maybe she got a tutor for Spanish class. She was having a hard time with verb tenses. Or maybe she –"

"There's one way we can find out exactly what it is," Felicia suggested.

"You mean ask her?" I guessed.

"No. She'd never tell us anyway," Felicia said. "We have to see if that website you use all the time has a quiz that can help us figure it out."

I knew exactly which website she meant. It was called middleschoolsurvival.com and it had lots of really cool info on it. There were all these quizzes that told you about you and your friends. So far, the quizzes on the website had been right on target. Felicia was right. Maybe it could help us figure out what was up with Chloe.

I turned on my computer, opened up my favorites list, and clicked on middleschoolsurvival.com. Then I scanned the contents of the site. "Here's a perfect one," I said. "It's called ***Is She Hiding Something . . . or Someone?***"

"Great. What's the first question?" Felicia asked excitedly.

1. Has your pal been especially secretive lately?

   - Yes
   - No

"That one's easy," Felicia said. "She's been really secretive. Click yes."

2. Have you noticed a change in her appearance lately? Is she dressing more stylishly, or with a few extra accessories?

   - Yes
   - No

I thought about the jeans and t-shirt Chloe was wearing at lunch today. The shirt said 4/3 OF PEOPLE HAVE TROUBLE WITH FRACTIONS. It was pretty funny, but she'd worn it a few times this year already. And the only accessory Chloe ever had was her backpack, which I didn't think counted.

"That's a no," I told Felicia, as I clicked the mouse.

3. Does your friend seem to be in an especially good mood – singing in the halls or smiling a lot?

- Yes
- No

"Yes! Yes!" Felicia squealed excitedly. "Chloe is singing all the time these days."

"That's because she's in the show," I told Felicia.

"The question doesn't ask why," Felicia reminded me. "It just asks if she's doing it. And she is."

I couldn't argue with that. I clicked the yes button.

4. Has your mysterious bud been disappearing more often than usual?

- Yes
- No

"That one's a yes, I guess," I told Felicia. "She's never around outside of school anymore."

"I know, I tried calling her before I called you tonight, but she didn't answer her cell," Felicia replied. "She always answers her cell."

That answered that. I clicked the yes button.

5. Has your friend been listening to a lot of love songs these days?

- Yes
- No

"All Chloe's been listening to lately is the soundtrack for *You're a Good Man, Charlie Brown*," I told Felicia. "She has to learn the songs for the show. She's in the chorus, but she also has that solo during the song 'Suppertime.'"

"That's definitely not a love song," Felicia agreed. "It's about dog food."

I giggled. "That's a no then." I said, clicking my mouse.

A moment later, the results of the quiz popped up on my screen.

You have answered Yes to three out of five questions.

Mostly Yes answers: Your pal is definitely hiding something. An air of romance seems to be surrounding her. Be patient. She's sure to tell you all about it as soon as she feels secure in her new relationship.

Mostly No answers: Your friend may be keeping a secret, but it's doubtful there's a new Mr. Right in her life at the moment. You may want to let her know you're there to talk if she feels like sharing some info about what's up.

"Yeah! I was right!" Felicia exclaimed excitedly. "Chloe's totally in love."

I laughed. Felicia sure loved being right about things. She sounded like she'd just won a million dollars or something.

"I wonder who it is," she continued.

"The quiz says we have to be patient and let her tell us when she's ready," I reminded her.

"I hate being patient," Felicia said with a groan.

"Me too. But we don't have any choice. Chloe's not going to tell us anything before she's ready." I paused for a minute. "And you can't tell anyone, either. We have to keep Chloe's secret, a secret."

"Agreed," Felicia said. "This is just between us."

Chapter THREE

"What theater-crowd diva has a new love in her life? Seems one constantly singing sixth-grade superstar-wannabe is hiding a new man – even from her closest friends."

I sat at our lunch table and stared at the very first gossip column in the *Joyce Kilmer Gazette* in amazement. It was called "In the Know with Madame X." That gossip had to be about Chloe. Who else could it be?

But no one knew that Chloe was hiding a secret love – except Felicia and me.

"Yo, Jenny, did you see this?" Marilyn asked as she came over to the table. She was holding up the newspaper.

"It's gotta be Chloe," Carolyn said. "She's the only sixth-grader who sings all the time."

I looked up at the twins. They were both wearing the same green polo shirts and faded blue jeans. "What's up with the clothes?" I asked them.

"I had a math test second period today," Carolyn explained. (At least I thought it was Carolyn. It was hard to tell who was who when the twins dressed the same).

"What does a math test have to do with your clothes?" I wondered out loud.

But before Marilyn or Carolyn could explain it to me, Liza looked up and shook her head. "I hope you guys don't get caught this time," Liza said. "Remember what happened last year?"

"What happened?" I asked. "What are you guys talking about?"

"Señorita Gonzalez caught me taking her Spanish test," Carolyn explained, pointing to her sister.

"When our mom found out, she threatened to make me dye my hair red so the teachers could tell us apart," Marilyn continued. "Can you imagine what I'd look like with red hair?" She turned to her sister. "She should have wanted you to dye *your* hair. I think you'd look much better as a redhead."

I laughed at that. The twins were identical. Neither one of them would have looked particularly hot with red hair.

"Yeah. But we didn't get caught today," Carolyn pointed out. "I hope you got an A for me on that test."

"Well, I got a few wrong on purpose," Marilyn told her. "Otherwise your math teacher would have suspected something." She turned to Liza and me. "Can we get back to this Chloe situation?" she asked.

"Yeah," Marilyn agreed. "Who do you think this guy is?"

"We don't know that there is a guy, or that this diva is Chloe," Liza reminded her.

"Come on, who else can it be?" Marc asked, coming up behind the twins and putting his tray on the table.

"So you saw the article too," Liza said.

Marc nodded. "Everyone has. Madame X's article is all anyone's talking about. It's the first time there's ever been a gossip column in the school paper."

"You really think the article's about Chloe?" I asked.

Marc shrugged. "Could be."

"You live next door to her . . ." Carolyn began.

" . . . have you seen any new guys around her house?" Marilyn finished her sister's thought.

"Just her dad," Marc said. "I saw him waiting for her in their front yard when we got home from school."

Liza giggled. "I don't think that's what they meant."

"If you want to know if it's true, why don't you just ask Chloe?" Marc suggested to the twins.

"Ask Chloe what?" Chloe said, as she walked over to our table with Josh.

"Um . . . uh . . . nothing," Marilyn said, quickly slipping the school paper onto her lap.

"Yeah. We, um, forgot what we were talking about," Carolyn added.

"You *both* forgot?" Josh asked. "Isn't that taking the twin thing a little too far?"

"It wasn't anything important," Liza told Chloe. "Just stupid gossip."

"Oh," Chloe replied. "I hate that. Why don't you guys leave the gossip to the Pops? That's what they do best."

As if on cue, Addie and Dana walked right past our table. They stopped for a minute and stood behind Chloe.

"*Mwah!*" Dana said, making a big kissing noise.

Addie giggled and kissed at the air. "Oh, lover boy. You handsome mystery man."

Dana began laughing hysterically as she and Addie walked off toward their table.

"What was that about?" Chloe asked, once the Pops were out of earshot.

"You're kidding, right?" Marc asked her.

Chloe shook her head. "Nope. Haven't a clue what those two were babbling about."

"Then you haven't seen the paper today?" I asked her.

"What paper?"

"This paper," Marc said, pulling his copy of the *Joyce Kilmer Gazette* from his backpack. As he handed it to Chloe, he pulled his video camera out. Obviously he wanted to get Chloe's reaction to the story on tape.

"Oh, Marc, don't," Liza pleaded.

But it was too late. Chloe was already staring at Madame X's gossip column. As she read, her eyes opened wide.

"Now, Chloe, don't get upset," Liza said gently.

"Yeah, they don't mention your name or anything," I added. "Probably hardly anyone knows it's about you."

Chloe didn't say anything. Instead, she took a deep breath. Her hands began to shake ever so slightly, and her cheeks turned a slight pink. Then she opened her mouth wide and . . .

She laughed. Chloe *laughed.* Like the whole article was the funniest thing she'd ever seen.

"Everyone thinks this is about me?" she asked us between giggles.

"Isn't it?" I asked.

"If I have a boyfriend, it's news all right," Chloe said. "News to me!"

"Then it's not true?" I asked.

Chloe shook her head. "Of course not. Why would you guys think that?"

"Well you've been acting kind of weird lately," Liza told her.

"What are you talking about?" Chloe asked.

"Like when you wouldn't go to our house after school the other day," Marilyn told her.

"Even after you found out there was no rehearsal," Carolyn added.

Chloe shrugged. "I was busy."

"And then you didn't want to go dress shopping with Felicia, Rachel, and me," I reminded her.

"I didn't say I didn't *want* to go, I said I *couldn't* go," Chloe said. She bit her lip and looked down at her hands. "It's not the same thing."

"But you didn't say *why* you couldn't go," I explained.

"And just because of that you thought I had a boyfriend?" Chloe sounded incredulous. "You guys have huge imaginations."

"Well, you have to admit your behavior's been kind of strange the past few days," Liza said gently.

"It's totally felt like you're hiding something," I added.

Chloe sighed. "I have been hiding something," she admitted finally. "But it's not what you think."

Marc turned off his camera and looked over at her. "What's up, Chloe?" he asked, quietly.

Chloe sighed. "I didn't want to tell you guys, because I don't need anybody feeling bad for me."

"Just tell us," Josh said. "We'll be cool about it, whatever it is. Promise."

Chloe took a deep breath. "Well, the thing is, my dad lost his job two weeks ago," she blurted out. "And money's kind of tight. That's why I couldn't go shopping with you guys," she told me. "I can't afford any new clothes right now."

"Wow," I said quietly. "That stinks."

"It's no big deal. Dad's already had a few interviews, and he'll get something soon. But right now, I can't just go out and buy new stuff," Chloe explained.

"Yeah, but what does that have to do with coming to our house?" Marilyn asked her.

"Hanging out with us wouldn't have cost you anything," Carolyn added.

"Yeah, but my mom's working overtime a lot right now. So whenever I don't have rehearsal, I feel like I should go home and help out with the cooking and cleaning and stuff," Chloe told the twins.

Boy, did I feel stupid. Here Chloe was going through all this, and I'd been convinced she'd had a boyfriend. Why had I listened to Felicia?

Felicia! Boy, was I mad at her. She and I had been the only two people who had suspected Chloe had a boyfriend. I was pretty sure of that. Which could mean only one thing, Felicia had broken her promise to keep the results of that quiz secret. She'd blabbed to Madame X.

Because of that, everyone in school thought Chloe had some mystery boyfriend. And she'd had to tell us this horrible secret about her dad.

Not that Chloe seemed too upset about that. "Actually, I'm kind of glad you all know now," she said. "It really stunk having to lie to you like that."

"I wish you could have a new outfit for the dance," I told her.

"Me, too," Chloe said with a sigh. "Oh, well."

"Maybe you can earn the money," Liza suggested. "You could get a part-time job or something, on the days when you don't have rehearsals."

"I'm too young to get a job," Chloe said.

"Yeah, you have to be fifteen or sixteen to work in a store," Josh said.

"Well, there are kid jobs," Marc said. "Like delivering newspapers or something."

"You have to do that early in the morning," Chloe reminded him. "I can hardly get up for school as it is."

"There has to be something you can do," I told her. Then I got a great idea. "I know just where to find the perfect job. Call me as soon as you get home!"

* * *

My cell phone began to ring five minutes after I walked into my house that afternoon. I checked the caller ID. Chloe. Awesome! Now she and I could get started on her dance outfit fund.

"Hey, Chloe," I said. "Let me just turn on the computer, and we can get started right away."

"You're going to that website that helped you decide if you should run for class president?" she asked.

"Yup," I told her. "It's the website that helped Felicia and me figure out that Josh really liked her. And it's also the site that helped us figure out the Josh wasn't spying on us for the Pops during my presidential campaign."

"That site is amazing." Chloe said. "It's never wrong."

Well, that wasn't exactly true. That last quiz Felicia and I had tried had said Chloe had a secret boyfriend. But I didn't tell Chloe that. She would've been mad that we'd butted into her business. Besides, it wasn't like the website had been *totally* wrong. It did say that Chloe had a secret. It was just the wrong secret.

"Okay, here's a good one," I said finally, after logging onto the site and scanning the list of quizzes. "Are You Ready for Your First Job?"

"Perfect!" Chloe exclaimed. "Read me the first question. The sooner we get going, the sooner I'll have the cash for a new outfit."

I laughed. It was funny to hear Chloe get so excited about getting clothes. I'd never thought of her as the kind of person to care about how she looked.

I guess that was just another secret she was hiding from me.

1. Which of these best describes you?

A. Little kid person
B. Pet person
C. Book person
D. People person

Chloe thought about that for a moment before answering. "Well, I like people," she said. "But I also love dogs and little kids. Can we check all three?"

"Nope."

"All right," she said. "Then click Pet person. I like animals. They love you no matter what."

"Cool," I said, clicking B. "Next question."

2. Which is your strongest personality trait?

A. Patient and calm
B. Responsible and careful
C. Organized and detailed
D. Open-minded and free-spirited

"Oh, that's easy," Chloe said. "I'm totally open about everything."

I frowned slightly before I tapped the D. After all, Chloe

hadn't been so open about her dad being out of work. But I guess that was sort of *his* secret, and she was honoring it.

3. What is most important to you in life?

A. Human contact
B. Unconditional love
C. Mental stimulation
D. To be worshipped

"That's a tough one," Chloe said. "I like being around some people, like you guys. But being around the Pops and people like that make me sick. I guess my answer would have to be B."

"Good choice," I said, clicking the B.

4. What's your favorite subject in school?

A. History
B. Phys ed
C. Science
D. Public speaking

"Too bad they didn't give lunch as a choice." Chloe giggled. "But if I have to choose one, I guess it's history. I liked learning about ancient Egypt. The pyramids and mummies are cool."

"A it is," I said. "Okay, here's the last question."

5. What was your favorite childhood game or activity?

A. Finger painting

B. Tag

C. Reading

D. King of the mountain

"I still love to play tag," Chloe admitted. "I know it's kinda babyish, but I play with my little cousin and her friends all the time. Don't tell anyone, okay?"

"Your secret's safe with me," I assured her. I clicked the Submit Your Answers icon.

A moment later the results popped up on the screen.

You answered 2 A's, 2 B's, and 1 D.

Here's what your results mean:

Mostly A's: As a calm, cool, person who is totally in touch with her inner toddler, a career in teaching may be your best bet. Kids would benefit from your patience and genuine love of fun.

Mostly B's: For you, a life without animals would be just too rough. Consider a career as a veterinarian or a zoologist.

Mostly C's: You're a definite brainiac who tends to be happiest on your own. A career in medical research or computer science would fit your temperament.

Mostly D's: You thrive on being the center of attention in a crowd of your peers. Consider a career in publicity or sales, and you've got it made!

"Well, you got two A's and two B's," I noted. "So that means you can be either a veterinarian or a teacher."

"I always knew I was versatile," Chloe said. "With my personality I can do just about anything."

I laughed. Chloe might be great with dogs and little kids, but she wasn't good at being modest. Of course, that was what made Chloe, Chloe. We all loved her for it.

"Unfortunately, this quiz isn't going to help me get a new outfit for the dance," Chloe continued. "You can't be a teacher or a veterinarian when you're only eleven years old."

"That's true," I agreed, frowning. Then, suddenly, I brightened. "Maybe you can't be a vet just yet," I told Chloe. "But this definitely gives me an idea!"

Chapter FOUR

CHLOE'S

Dog Walking and Grooming

Available after school on Fridays.

$2 for a walk

$3 for a walk and bath

Call 555-4323

I USED EXTRA-STRONG TAPE to post the sign on the wooden post near our school bus stop the next morning. I had a whole stack of them in my backpack. I was going to post some in school and then give the rest to Chloe and the twins to put up in their neighborhoods. Between the four of us I figured we had enough neighbors with dogs to get Chloe new clothes in no time!

"Oh, you're never going to believe this," Addie said into her cell phone. "Chloe's starting a dog walking service." She giggled. "This I gotta see."

I scowled, but didn't say anything. It wasn't worth it. I refused to give her the satisfaction of thinking that I would even *want* to eavesdrop on her conversation – again.

The bus came a moment later, and I hopped on. I saw Felicia sitting in the middle of the bus, but I took a seat up front, near Addie. I was too mad at Felicia for telling Madame X that Chloe had a boyfriend to sit next to her.

"Hey, Jenny, over here," I heard Felicia call to me.

I ignored her. I had nothing to say. Who knew what she'd blab next?

As the bus drove off, I sat by myself. I couldn't help but listen to Addie, who was sitting right behind me, go on and on to Dana about some Pops sleepover they were having on Friday night.

"I'll bring the new manicure kit my aunt sent me," I heard Addie say. She was quiet for a minute as Dana spoke. Then she started to laugh. "Well, if Claire would just stop biting her nails, she'd be able to use it, too. I swear, it's so disgusting the way she chews them and spits them out. What boy would ever want to hold her hand after that?"

Unbelievable! Claire was Addie's close friend. But here she was making fun of her with Dana . . .

MIDDLE SCHOOL RULE # 13:

NEVER TURN YOUR BACK ON THE POPS —
EVEN IF YOU *ARE* ONE!

As soon as the bus came to a halt at the next stop, Felicia came bounding up to the front of the bus. She plopped down in the seat beside me.

"Are you mad at me or something?" she asked.

"I don't know," I told her. "Should I be?"

"What's that supposed to mean?" Felicia wondered.

"I mean, did you do anything that might make me mad at you?" I asked her. "Like maybe telling Madame X our secret conversation about Chloe?"

"Who said I did that?" Felicia demanded.

"Well, somebody told her," I said. "And it was just you and me taking that quiz."

"So how do I know *you* didn't tell Madame X that Chloe has a boyfriend?" Felicia asked me.

"Because I don't even know who Madame X is," I told her. "And I would never tell Chloe's secret."

"I don't know who Madame X is, either," Felicia insisted. "And I can keep a secret as well as you. I would never have told anyone that Chloe Samson has a boyfriend!"

Just then, everyone on the bus got really quiet. Felicia had said that last part really loudly.

"She does not," I said just as loudly, so everyone on the bus could hear. I wanted to make sure that no more rumors were spread about Chloe. Then I whispered again. "She has a secret, but that's not it."

"What is it?" Felicia asked me.

I shook my head, hard. "I'm not spilling any of Chloe's secrets."

"But I swear, I didn't tell anyone about the boyfriend quiz," Felicia said. She made an X on her chest. "Cross my heart and hope to die."

She sounded really sincere. But I couldn't be sure. And besides, it wasn't up to me to talk about Chloe's dad. If she wanted to tell Felicia, that was her business.

Still, if there was a chance that Felicia hadn't been the one to tell Madame X about Chloe, then I probably shouldn't be mad at her. I'd have to believe she was telling the truth.

In the background I could hear Addie talking on her cell phone, telling Dana about how Felicia and I were fighting.

"It's an all-out geek fight." Addie giggled into her phone.

That was enough to make me stop arguing with Felicia. I reached into my backpack and pulled out one of Chloe's flyers.

"Maybe you want to bring Bruno over for a walk and

bath tomorrow?" I suggested. Bruno was Felicia's dog. He was a big, furry mutt that everyone loved.

Felicia looked down and read the flyer. "Sure," she said. "He could use a bath. He was rolling around in the grass all afternoon yesterday." She thought for a moment. "Does this dog thing have anything to do with Chloe's real secret?"

I laughed. Felicia wasn't giving up so easily.

"Well, it is somewhat related," I said. "But I can honestly tell you that Chloe's secret has nothing to do with dogs. It's purely a people thing."

"So, how many dogs do we have?" I asked Chloe as we walked to English class together the next morning. It was Friday, and our dog adventure was scheduled for that afternoon.

"I got four calls. One from Felicia, one from Marc, and the other two were my mother's friends, Mrs. Miller and Mrs. Donahue," Chloe replied. "Mrs. Miller's dog, Barney, just needs a walk. But Marc said we can give Skippy a bath. Which should be easy, because he's just a little cocker spaniel. Mrs. Donahue wants us to bathe Chester also. He's a schnauzer and not too big. Bruno's gonna be the tough one. That dog's huge."

"We can handle him," I told her. "Remember, there will be four of us, and only one of him."

"It's really nice of you, Marilyn, and Carolyn to help me with this," Chloe said.

"It'll be fun," I told her. "What time are we getting started?"

"Right after school. I'll pick Skippy up on my way home, and then you and the twins can take turns picking up the other dogs. When we have all four of them, we can take them on their walk."

"Sounds like a plan," I said.

"I figured it all out. Today we'll earn eleven dollars," Chloe said. "But I was thinking that you guys are doing so much work, we should really split the money."

"We can figure all of that out after you have enough money to get whichever dress you want for the dance," I told her.

"A few afternoons of doggie day care should earn me enough money," Chloe said.

"Awesome!" I said.

"And I owe it all to you," Chloe said gratefully. She paused for a minute and then added, "Well, you and middleschoolsurvival.com."

"Okay, here's Barney," I said, as I brought the brown-and-black German Shepherd mix into Chloe's backyard later that day.

"I've got Chester and Skippy here already," Chloe added, gesturing with the two leashes she held in her hand. "And the twins should be here any second with Bruno."

I nodded. We had decided that it would probably take

two of us to walk Bruno, since he was so huge, and sometimes he pulled on his leash pretty hard.

"I think we should take all four dogs for their walks first," I told Chloe. "Then, I can take Barney home while you and the twins start the baths."

"Good idea," Chloe said. "I've got all the doggie shampoo ready to go in the upstairs bathroom."

Just then, Marilyn, Carolyn, and Bruno came bounding into the yard. Bruno was pulling so hard on his leash that Marilyn, who was holding on to the other end, was practically flying in the air like a kite.

"Bruno, stop!" Marilyn cried. "Stop!"

But Bruno didn't stop. He just kept running around and around the yard at top speed – until Chloe pulled a bone-shaped dog cookie from her pocket.

"Bruno, sit!" she said firmly, holding up the cookie. Bruno did as he was told. He sat back on his hind legs and looked up eagerly at Chloe. She smiled and held out the cookie. Bruno gobbled it up in a second, and then sat there, staring at her adoringly.

"Wow!" I exclaimed. "The website was right. You do have a talent for working with animals."

"It's all about the food." Chloe giggled. "Okay you guys, let's go for our walks."

"Can you take Bruno?" Marilyn asked. "We're tired just from walking him here."

"Actually, it's more like he was walking us," Carolyn added.

"Fine. I'll take Bruno," Chloe said. She took his leash and then handed Skippy and Chester to the twins.

"Why don't we take them to the park?" I suggested as we left the backyard and headed down the street. "Dogs love parks."

"And fire hydrants," Chloe said, laughing as Bruno stopped at a red hydrant and lifted his leg.

"This is kind of fun," Marilyn said, as Chester walked cheerfully at her side.

"Good exercise, too," Carolyn agreed. "Mom would be happy."

I nodded in agreement. All moms have a thing about going out and getting some fresh air. I guess it's a parent thing.

"It sure is easier walking a little dog," Carolyn continued.

"You seem to have Bruno under control, though," Marilyn told Chloe. "I don't know how you're doing it."

Just then, Skippy started to bark. Marilyn jumped.

"He spotted a squirrel, that's all," Chloe told her. "No big deal."

But the squirrel *was* a big deal – to Skippy, anyway. A moment later, the little cocker spaniel yanked on his leash and took off after it. Marilyn was so surprised by how strong the little guy was that she dropped the leash, and Skippy ran off at top speed to chase the squirrel. Marilyn stood there, frozen.

"Don't just stand there, go get him!" Chloe shouted at her.

"I, I . . .I . . . he's so fast," Marilyn stammered.

"I'll get him!" I shouted, handing Barney's leash to Marilyn. I darted off after Skippy.

Boy, he was a speedy little cocker spaniel! Before I knew what had happened, Skippy had turned the corner and chased the squirrel across someone's front lawn. I ran right behind him. "Stop! Skippy!" I yelled. Then I remembered Chloe's trick. "Skippy, stop! Cookie?"

But Skippy was far more interested in the squirrel than a cookie. He kept on running, going under a hole in the fence and into another backyard. I scrambled to open the back gate, not caring that I didn't even know the people who lived there.

The squirrel raced up a tree. Skippy sat beneath it, barking wildly and leaping up and down.

Now was my chance. I hurried over to the tree, and reached for Skippy's leash. As soon as I had it in my hands, I shouted, "Gotcha!"

My shout must have scared Skippy because he started running at top speed. But there was no way he was going to get away again. I held that leash tight and ran as fast as I could until . . . *boom!* I tripped over a tree root and fell flat on my stomach. Skippy scampered for a few more feet, but I held tight, steeling myself to the ground like the anchor of a ship. When the leash couldn't stretch any farther, Skippy finally gave up.

"Skippy, I can't believe you did that!" I scolded him. Skippy looked up at me and cocked his head. Then he gave me a big doggie smile. Okay, maybe he was just thirsty or something, but it *looked* like a smile. And it melted my heart. "Okay, come on. Let's go find everybody else."

Skippy and I walked out of the yard and quickly made our way to the sidewalk. We began heading back around the corner, to where we'd left Chloe, the twins, and the other three dogs.

Just as we turned the corner, THEY appeared. Claire and Dana. In all their Pops perfection.

And there I was, covered in mud and all sweaty from chasing Skippy around some stranger's backyard.

"Nice look," Claire said, studying my grass-stained jeans and muddy T-shirt.

"I especially like the tree branch stuck in your hair," Dana added with a giggle. "You look like some sort of monster."

"Like Swamp Thing!" Claire added, laughing harder.

Just then, Skippy started to bark wildly. It wasn't a friendly bark, either. He was growling, and pulling on his leash.

"Whoa! Get that rabid dog away from me." Claire gulped, then she ran off with Dana hurrying right behind her.

People always say that dogs can sense when someone is mean or dangerous. Obviously Skippy had figured out how awful Claire and Dana were just by looking at them. He didn't care if they were Pops. He just knew he wanted no part of them. "Smart dog," I said with a grin as I patted his head. "It took me weeks to figure that out."

Just then, Chloe and Bruno came bounding over to us. "We heard all the barking," Chloe said. "Is everything okay?"

I nodded. "Skippy's a fast runner, but I caught him," I told her proudly.

"I think it's time to go home and give the dogs their baths now," Chloe suggested.

I looked down at my grass-stained clothing and muddy hands. "They're not the only ones who need a bath," I said with a laugh.

"How much of this stuff should we put in the water?" Carolyn asked as she, Chloe, and I started to fill the bathtub in Chloe's upstairs bathroom. Her parents weren't home, so we were on our own. Marilyn had gone to return Barney to Mrs. Miller. That left the three of us to give the other dogs their baths.

"Lots," I said. "Skippy is filthy from running around that yard."

"Bruno doesn't smell a whole lot better," Carolyn pointed out.

"I think we should start with Bruno," Chloe suggested. "He's the biggest, and he'll probably take the longest to dry."

"Cool." I picked up the bottle of dog shampoo, poured in plenty, and turned up the water. Before long the tub was three-quarters of the way filled with bubbling, soapy water. "You can put him in now," I told Chloe.

"Okay. Come on, Bruno," Chloe said, tapping the side of the tub. "In you go."

But Bruno didn't budge. He just stood there in the center of the bathroom floor.

"Bruno. In the water," Chloe said in a firm voice.

Bruno lay down on the floor and covered his head with his front paws.

"We're gonna have to put him in there," Chloe said. She turned to Carolyn and me. "Come on. It'll take all three of us to lift him."

Even with three people lifting him up, Bruno was plenty heavy. But we managed to get him on his feet, and then with a couple of nudges and shoves, the big guy reluctantly jumped in.

Splash! I guess I'd filled the tub a little too high, because as soon as Bruno got in, buckets of foamy water overflowed out all over the bathroom floor.

"Oops," I said sheepishly.

"*Grrr,*" Bruno growled angrily. He obviously didn't feel like having a bath. But that was what Felicia's mother had paid for, and that was what we were going to give him. I began to soap his short brown fur.

Bruno shook his head really hard. Water flew all around the room.

"Whoa, what's going on in here?" Marilyn asked as she opened the door, stepping into the bathroom and taking in the wet, soapy floor, the flying bubbles, and the wet, angry dog.

"Close the door!" Carolyn shouted at her sister. But it was too late. As soon as Bruno sensed a means of escape, he took it, leaping out of the tub and running out into the hall.

Chloe hurried after him with a towel in hand, but it was too late. Bruno was already drying his soapy fur by rolling around wildly on the hall carpet.

"Bruno, stop!" Chloe shouted. "STOP! Not on the carpet!"

Surprisingly, Bruno stopped rolling on the carpet. He stood up and stared at Chloe. "That's better," she told him.

Bruno let out a loud yelp and raced into Chloe's parents' room. He leaped onto the bed, rolled over on his back, and began to wriggle around on the comforter.

"Oh, no!" Chloe shouted. "Bruno, get off of there before my mom or dad catch you on their . . ."

"What's going on in here?" Chloe's father shouted as he stormed into the bedroom. "Why is that wet dog on my bed?"

"We were giving him a bath," Chloe explained. "And he escaped."

"It was really my fault, Mr. Samson," Marilyn said. "If I hadn't opened the bathroom door . . ."

"We'll clean everything up, Dad, I promise," Chloe said.

"You bet you will," Mr. Samson said sternly. "Starting right now."

"Well, we still have two dogs to wash first, and then . . ." Chloe began.

Mr. Samson looked at the big wet stain on his comforter and shook his head. "No more dog baths, Chloe. As of this moment, your dog care company is officially out of business."

"WELL, AT LEAST YOU STILL got paid eight dollars for walking the dogs," I said to Chloe as she and I walked through C wing together Monday morning. "It's a start."

"And a finish," Chloe added. "You heard what my dad said about us being out of business."

"Well, there has to be another way for you to earn the rest of the money you need for that dress," I told her. "Rachel, Felicia, and I are determined to help you. That's why we decided not to go shopping this weekend. We're waiting for you to get enough money together and come with us."

Chloe opened up her mouth to speak. But her words were drowned out by Claire's furious screaming.

As usual, a few of the Pops had gathered at Addie's locker to put on their morning makeup. They did that every day. But today, instead of giggling and gossiping, Claire looked furious. More surprisingly, all that anger was focused on her fellow Pops, not us.

"I cannot believe you people. How could you?" she demanded.

"How could we what?" Dana asked her.

"Which one of you jerks did this?" Claire shouted at

the top of her lungs as she waved a copy of a newspaper in her hands. "Now the whole school will know."

"Must be the new edition of the *Joyce Kilmer Gazette*," Chloe said. "I'll bet there's something about Claire in Madame X's column."

"Whatever it is, Claire's really mad about it," I added.

"We have to get our hands on a copy of that newspaper," Chloe said, looking around the hall until she finally spotted a stack of school newspapers at the end of the hall. She darted toward them and picked up two copies, one for me and one for her.

"What pretty Pop still sucks her thumb in her sleep?" Chloe read aloud from Madame X's column. "It's starting to make her teeth stick out. Be careful, Bucky Beaver!"

Dana looked over at Elena Ross, a seventh-grade Pop who had become friendly with Claire last year and now hung out with Addie and Dana, too. "It must have been you," Dana said.

"You were at the sleepover Friday night, too," Elena reminded her. "You saw Claire sucking her thumb. We all did!"

"I don't know which one of you decided to let the whole school know I still suck my thumb, but right now I hate all of you!" Claire shouted, storming off.

Chloe shook her head. "Her name's not anywhere in the article. No one but the Pops who were at that slumber party would have known it was Claire in that article.

She just told the whole school herself that she was the thumb sucker. How dumb is that?!"

As Chloe and I headed down the hall, the Pops continued to argue.

"I didn't even notice she was doing it," Elena told Dana. "I was sleeping, too. Maybe it was Maya. She was at the party and you know how she loves to gossip."

"Maya? You really think?" Dana asked.

Elena shrugged. "It could have been her, or you, or even Addie here. All I know is that it wasn't me."

As I watched the Pops battling it out at Addie's locker, I was struck by an amazing thought. Whoever this Madame X was, she was now the most powerful person in the school. She'd made everyone in the school suspicious and nervous. Who would be next? Apparently, no one was safe. Not even the Pops.

"Okay, how weird is this?" Josh asked as he sat down at our table during lunch and looked around the cafeteria.

"Very weird," Liza agreed in her soft voice. "They're all over the place."

I knew exactly what Liza was talking about. The Pops were scattered all around the cafeteria, instead of sitting at their usual star-studded table by the windows. Addie was with a boy named Sean from the eighth grade, a few tables away from me and my friends. Dana was sitting all by herself, pretending to read a book, while

Elena and Aaron were at the usual Pops table, and Claire and Jeffrey were over by the juice machine.

"This is great," Marc said, as he held up his camera and filmed each of the new Pop locations. "It's adding real drama to my film."

"Boy, that Madame X is something," Josh said. "With one sentence she can bring the Pops to their knees."

"It's only because the Pops are letting her get to them," Liza said quietly. "If people just ignored her column, she wouldn't have any power."

I looked admiringly at Liza. She was shy, and she didn't talk a lot, but the few things she said were pretty amazing.

"Well, I, for one, am really grateful to Madame X," Chloe told us.

Considering one of the rumors Madame X had started had been about her, I thought that was kind of a strange thing for Chloe to say. "You are?" I asked with surprise.

"Oh, yeah," Chloe said with a grin. "For once we'll have the girls' room all to ourselves during lunch!"

I had to laugh. Chloe was right. From the looks of things, there would be no meeting of the Pop gossip committee in the girls' bathroom today.

"Whoa, check that out," Marc said, moving his camera over toward where Claire was sitting. "What is she doing?"

At that moment, Claire leaped up on a cafeteria table, and blew a whistle – loud!

"Everyone, can I have your attention!" she shouted.

Of course everyone in the room grew quiet.

MIDDLE SCHOOL RULE # 14:

WHEN POPS TALK, PEOPLE LISTEN.

"I just wanted to fill all of you in on some things that didn't make Madame X's column!" Claire shouted. "There's one Pop girl in this school who sews designer labels into her discount store clothes."

"Big deal," Chloe said. "Who cares about that?"

Apparently Elena did, because she jumped up from her seat and started shouting. "I only did that once!" she insisted. "And anyway, I'm not the only one. Everyone knows Dana's Kate Spade bag is a fake. Her dad got it for her from a street vendor in the city!"

Now it was Dana's turn to get angry. "Yeah, well, at least I don't kiss my Lenny Charles poster before I go to bed every night!"

No one had to tell me which Pop that was. Addie'd had a crush on Lenny Charles ever since we'd first seen him on TV. Not that I blamed her. He was definitely the cutest guy on TV. If I had a poster with his picture on it, I'd probably kiss it, too.

But Dana hadn't been talking about me. She'd been

talking about Addie. Still, even as Addie's cheeks turned bright red, she didn't say a word. She was too smart to admit that that rumor was about her.

"Oh, horrors!" Liza whispered, giggling. "A fake purse and a crush on a movie star. How terrible."

I laughed. Liza was right. It was hard to believe the stupid things the Pops took seriously. And apparently, I wasn't the only one who thought so. Other people were snickering too, people who ordinarily wouldn't have had the guts to laugh at the Pops – at least not to their faces. But this look into how petty and ridiculous their world was definitely made people a little more brave.

I wondered how long it would last.

"I heard you guys had a really good time at lunch," Rachel said as I ran into her in the school parking lot at the end of the day. "Man, I wish I had fifth-period lunch."

"Me, too," Felicia agreed. "The only exciting thing that happened during our lunch was that Michael Newman dropped his tray."

"Not exactly Madame X - newsworthy," Rachel noted.

"Yeah, our lunch was definitely more exciting than that," I said. "The Pops were totally out of control."

"I'm telling you, things are getting weird around here," Rachel said.

Just then, as if on cue, Addie walked over to where

Rachel, Felicia, and I were standing. She had a friendly smile on her face.

Rachel was right. Things were *definitely* getting weirder by the moment!

"Um, Jenny," she said. "Are you free after school today?"

Huh?

Addie didn't seem to notice my confused, silent stare. "Because if you are," she continued, "maybe we could stay and work on the menu for the luau and take the late bus home together?"

I wasn't quite sure what to say. That was probably the nicest Addie had been to me all school year. Of course, it was probably only because all her real friends were fighting and she had nothing to do after school, but still, it was nice to hear her sounding human.

Besides, the luau was coming up and things had to get done. And as class president it was my job to make sure that happened.

"Sure, no problem," I said. "I'll meet you in the student council room in a few minutes. I just need to talk to Rachel and Felicia first."

"Oh," Addie said. She sounded a bit surprised that I wasn't going to just dump my friends right then and run off after her. "Sure. I'll meet you there."

As Addie walked off, Felicia shook her head in amazement. "Weird, huh?" she said.

I nodded. "Listen, let's talk later tonight. We still have to help Chloe come up with an idea to make money to buy that dress."

"You're right," Rachel said. "I'll call you guys and Chloe later."

I nodded. Rachel was the only one of us who could do conference calling on her phone. "About eight thirty?" I suggested.

"Cool," Rachel agreed. "Hey, do you guys know how the two telephones got married?"

"How?" Felicia asked, rolling her eyes slightly.

"In a double *ring* ceremony," Rachel answered, chuckling. "Get it?"

"Yeah, and we're giving it back," Felicia told her. "Come on, we're gonna miss our bus." She turned to me. "Good luck with Addie. I hope it's not too terrible."

"Thanks," I said. "Me, too."

"Hi, Jenny," Addie said in a voice that was so friendly I was tempted to look around the student council office for the hidden cameras.

But Addie wasn't punking me. She was genuinely glad to see me. I could tell by her eyes. They looked sort of happy, instead of angry, which was how she usually looked when I was around.

"Uh . . . hi." I answered cautiously.

"I've set everything up," Addie said, pointing to the

various piles around the room. "These paper flowers are for stringing the leis. We should give one out to everyone as they come in. I've already made a bunch. And then over there" – she pointed to a big box under the desk – "are the blow-up palm trees and beach balls. I ordered them real cheap from a catalogue, so they aren't breaking our budget or anything. And then over there are the limbo sticks and . . ."

As Addie went on and on about the directions for the luau, I had to hand it to her. She'd really made the most of the budget I'd given her. This was going to be the most amazing dance Joyce Kilmer Middle School had ever seen. Addie definitely had her talents. One of which was her ability to make the person she was talking to feel like the most important person in the world.

But why was she being so friendly to *me*? Just this morning she'd completely ignored me at the bus stop. And now she was acting like we were still best buds.

A couple of weeks ago I wouldn't have even bothered to question it. I would've been grateful for whatever crumbs of friendship she threw in my direction. But that was then. This was now. And now I had plenty of my own friends. I didn't need Addie in my life the way I used to; she'd changed too much.

Besides, Addie was totally using me. Thanks to Madame X, none of her friends were talking to each other. Which meant Addie had no one to hang out with after school. I guess as far as she was concerned, I was better than no one.

Not much of a compliment, huh?

I sat down and began stringing pink, white, and green flowers onto a cord. I pretended to focus really hard on what I was doing so I didn't have to talk to Addie anymore. I felt kind of uncomfortable sitting in the room, just the two of us and all.

"Oh, that's a pretty pattern," Addie complimented me.

"Thanks," I said, picking up some more flowers.

"This is fun, isn't it?" Addie continued. "Sort of like that time your mom bought you that new bead kit for Christmas, and we spent a whole snowstorm making jewelry, remember?"

Of course I remembered. I was just sort of shocked that she did. Addie always acted like she'd blocked out our whole friendship.

"So how's Felicia doing these days?" Addie asked me cheerfully. "I hardly ever see her anymore."

That's because you were so mean to her at camp last summer, I thought to myself. But out loud I said, "She's great. She and Rachel are on the basketball team. They might even make varsity."

"Wow, as sixth-graders? That's huge," Addie said. She paused for a minute, thinking. "How does Josh feel about Felicia maybe making varsity?"

"Josh?" I asked with a shrug. "I guess he's happy about it."

"It must be weird for him to have a girlfriend who is so good at sports, when he's not so great," Addie explained.

"Yeah, but he's amazing at other things," I defended him. "He helps Felicia with her homework sometimes."

"Mmm-hmm," Addie murmured. "You know, I noticed none of the guys you hang around with are great at sports."

The only other guy I hung around with was Marc, so I figured that was who she meant.

"Marc's okay at soccer and baseball, but he's so into his movie that –"

"He's making a movie? That's awesome," Addie interrupted. "Is he an actor?"

I shook my head. "No. He wants to be a director. He has this video camera he carries around, and he uses it to film stuff."

"What kind of stuff?"

"Middle school life," I said. "His movie's sort of like *The Real World*, except about *our* world."

"Sounds interesting."

"I guess so. He hasn't let any of us see it yet."

"Artists can be so independent," Addie noted.

I nodded. "You're not kidding. Liza's the same way. Chloe told me she won't let anyone help her paint the play scenery she's responsible for. She wants it to be absolutely perfect."

Addie chuckled. "She sounds like Claire. She won't let anyone touch her makeup."

I smiled. I couldn't believe how easy it was talking to Addie. I could feel myself falling back into our old, relaxed ways.

I know it's kind of mean, but I was glad the Pops were fighting with each other. Their arguments had given me my old friend back. At least for a little while.

"I'm telling you guys, she was totally normal – even nice," I told Felicia, Rachel, and Chloe during our conference call later that night.

"Whatever you say," Chloe said.

"Maybe it wasn't actually Addie," Rachel joked. "Did you pull on her face to see if it was real skin or just a mask?"

"Ha ha," I replied sarcastically. "This is real life, Rach, not *Mission Impossible*."

"Addie being that nice sounds utterly impossible," Felicia groaned.

"Whatever," I said finally. I was getting tired of defending Addie. Especially since I knew that by tomorrow morning she'd probably be back to her old new-self. "I thought we were going to figure out a way for Chloe to earn the rest of her money for that dress."

"Yeah," Chloe said. "That dog thing didn't work out so well."

"What else are you good at?" Rachel asked her.

"Talking," Felicia joked. "Too bad you can't make money doing that."

"I know," Chloe agreed with a laugh. "I'd be a millionaire by now."

"The website said you would be good at working with kids, too," I reminded Chloe. "Maybe there's something we could do with that."

"You could baby-sit," Rachel suggested.

"I wouldn't earn enough money in time," Chloe said.

"But if you baby-sit a few times . . ." Felicia began.

"There's not enough time," Chloe said. "I have only one free afternoon this week."

"What if you baby-sat for a couple of kids at once?" I suggested.

"That seems like a lot of responsibility. I can't imagine taking care of a few kids all at once."

"What if we all did it together?" I asked. "Sort of like a Thursday afternoon daycare. We could use my backyard for two hours. The kids could play there."

"Yeah," Rachel piped up. "Felicia and I could play sports with them."

"And I could do crafts," I said, remembering what Addie had said about the bead kit my mom had once given me. I still had tons of those beads left.

"And I could sing for them!" Chloe said.

"Or something," Felicia said quickly. "We'll think of some other activities."

"I'll make a few flyers tonight and post them around the neighborhood tomorrow before school," Chloe said. "Hopefully we'll get a bunch of kids by Thursday."

"I know we will!" I said confidently. "You'll have all the money you need. You'll see, Chloe."

Chapter SIX

TO AN OUTSIDER, things at our school might have seemed normal the next Tuesday morning. But even though they looked that way, they weren't normal at all. Everything was just a little bit off.

For starters, Addie was at her locker, putting on makeup, like always. But she was all alone. There was no crowd of Pops fighting for mirror time.

And, as usual, Claire was wearing a new shirt, and very trendy leather boots. But today, no one was enviously complimenting her on her new ensemble. In fact, Elena walked right past her without a word.

Dana was, as always, being mean to my friends and me.

"Nice T-shirt, Chloe," she said, sticking her finger down her throat and pretending to gag. "Where'd you get that thing? The Salvation Army?"

"Yes," said Chloe, but in the bizarre alternate reality my school had entered, Dana's slam fell on deaf ears. Without any of the other Pops there to laugh or add a mean comment of their own, no one cared at all about what she had to say.

I turned to Chloe and rolled my eyes. "Did you put up

any flyers on your way to the bus stop this morning?" I asked her, ignoring Dana completely.

Chloe nodded. "Yes, and I ran into my neighbor across the street, Mrs. Wilensky. She is dropping off her five-year-old, Julia, at four o'clock on Thursday."

"That's one kid already," I said enthusiastically. "And the signs haven't even been up for an hour."

"I know," Chloe said excitedly. "At this rate we could be millionaires in a month."

I laughed. Once again, Chloe was taking things to an extreme. "Come on, Bill Gates," I teased, dragging her by the arm. "We've got to get to English class."

"You're really going to go through with it?" I heard Felicia asking Rachel as I walked down C wing toward my locker at the end of the school day. The two of them were huddled by Felicia's locker, talking with Liza.

"Going through with what?" I asked curiously.

"Rachel's going to get a haircut tomorrow," Felicia told me.

"Actually, I'm going to get them all cut," Rachel joked.

"Ouch," Felicia said. "That one hurt."

"I want a completely different look," Rachel told me. "I'm so sick of this long, straight, red mop on my head. And I want to do it before the luau next week. I'm totally ready to look different."

I was really surprised to hear that. Ever since kindergarten, Rachel had had the same hairstyle. This was huge!

"I just don't know *how* I should get it cut," she said. "What style do you guys think would look best on me?"

I shrugged. "I usually just let the person who's cutting my hair decide," I said.

"I like my hair kind of short," Liza said. "That way it doesn't get in my way so much when I draw."

"Yeah, but I don't know if short hair would work on me," Rachel said. "And if I cut it short, I want to be sure it's right. Do you know how long it will take me to grow it out again if I don't like it?"

I nodded. A haircut was kind of a commitment.

"Do you think that website you go on might have some ideas?" Rachel asked me.

I shrugged. "It's got everything else," I said.

"Okay, I'll call you as soon as I get home from basketball practice so we can talk about the ideas we find," Rachel told me.

"Speaking of practice, I'd better get to the auditorium," Liza said suddenly.

"See ya later," I said as she turned to walk away.

"So be home around six o'clock," Rachel told me. "I'm dying to hear what that website says I should do about my hair."

That night, at six o'clock on the dot, my phone rang. "Did you find anything on the website?" Rachel asked me anxiously.

"Hello to you, too." I giggled.

"Oh, sorry," Rachel said. "Hi. I'm just so excited about this."

"I can tell," I said. I headed over to the computer and switched it on.

I typed in middleschoolsurvival.com and then searched the site for hairstyles. Sure enough, there was a section called Hairdos and Don'ts. I double-clicked the link and waited for the screen to load.

"Oh wow! This is everything you need!" I told Rachel excitedly. "But it's really long. Can I forward it to you instead of reading it over the phone?"

"That would be awesome!" Rachel exclaimed. "I'll force my brother to get off the computer."

"Okay, it's on its way," I said, attaching the information to an e-mail, and hitting Send.

"Thanks Jen, you're the best," Rachel said. After we hung up, I read over the information on the website. It was pretty cool. And I knew for sure it would help Rachel decide what to do.

Hairdos and Don'ts

When it comes to your hair, you have to take things at face value. Knowing which style will look good on you means having a sense of the shape of your face. Start by looking in the mirror. Pull your hair back and get close enough that you can see your face clearly reflected in the mirror. Then, use a lipstick to carefully outline your face on the mirror. Now step away. The shape you see drawn on the mirror is the shape of your face. (Be sure to have plenty of glass cleaner nearby. Your 'rents are sure to be miffed if they see lipstick all over the bathroom mirror!)

Once you've got the facial geometry down, here's how to make sure your style is a cut above.

OVAL-SHAPED FACE: Lucky you! People with oval-shaped faces can pretty much wear their hair any way they'd like. Let your hair's natural thickness and texture determine whether it works better long or short. (As a rule, if you have thin hair, keep it short and layered to add thickness.)

ROUND-SHAPED FACE: Keep the sides of your hair close to your face and add height at the crown of your head. This will soften the fullness of your face and give the illusion of a more oval-shaped face.

DIAMOND-SHAPED FACE: Narrow-faced girls need to give their faces a rounder look. Wide bangs with a chin-length bob will do the trick.

SQUARE-SHAPED FACE: The goal for you is to soften the angles of your face. This can easily be done with long, soft bangs that extend down over your temples. Your best bet is to have either long hair or short. Medium-length hairstyles won't accentuate your positives. Long hair should extend past the shoulder, while short haircuts should have some added height at the crown of your head to give your face a more oval look.

HEART-SHAPED FACE: Chin-length hairstyles, especially on girls with curly or wavy hair, will add fullness where it's needed. A side part will soften your chin.

Most important, don't get fooled into getting your hair cut in a certain way just because that's what's in style. Do what works best for your face. After all, as everyone knows, styles are hair today, gone tomorrow! ☺

The next day at lunch, everyone was talking about the dance. "I hope we don't have to eat a pig with an apple in its mouth at the luau," Chloe said as she took a bite of her peanut butter sandwich.

"It's not a real luau," I assured her. "We're serving pizza and ice cream sundaes. But we'll have Hawaiian pineapples, and punch served in plastic coconut shells."

"That sounds sooo cool," Chloe said, relieved.

"It was Addie's idea," I admitted with a shrug.

"She's good for something, I guess," Chloe replied.

"Hey, I just got some new face paints," Liza announced. "I can paint flowers on everyone's cheeks."

"Count me out," Marc said. "I'll just throw on a Hawaiian shirt, thanks."

"Me, too," Josh agreed.

Liza giggled. "I didn't mean you guys."

As I sat there in the lunchroom, I realized how many people were obsessing over Addie Wilson's Luau. That was what people were calling it. Not the School Luau. Or even the Sixth-Grade Luau. It was Addie's party. Plain and simple.

Not that I could argue with that. Our class vice president had pretty much done the whole thing by herself. And it did sound like it was going to be amazing.

I guess the thing that amazed me most was the effect the luau was having on my friends. They were almost as excited as the Pops were.

"Are you going with Rachel when she gets her hair cut today?" Chloe asked me.

I shook my head. "Too much homework. I have a math test on Friday. And since we're baby-sitting tomorrow after school . . ."

"How many kids do you guys have for that, anyway?" Josh asked.

"Four," Chloe said. "Not as many as I would've liked, but it's still pretty good."

"It's perfect," I assured her. "There are four of us to take care of four kids. I think we can handle that."

"I hope you handle it better than you handled the dogs," Marc teased.

"Yeah, maybe you should keep the kids on leashes, too," Marilyn added.

"Not like that helped with the dogs," Carolyn added with a laugh. "But seriously, I wish we could be there to help you guys. Unfortunately, we both have to go to the orthodontist."

"And we really do need to get rid of these retainers as soon as possible," Marilyn said, clicking hers up and down in her mouth.

"It's okay," I told the twins.

"Really," Chloe agreed. "We should be able to take care of a couple of little kids, easy."

I sighed heavily. I sure hoped Chloe was right. The last thing I wanted was a repeat of our dog day.

Chapter SEVEN

"WOW, RACHEL, YOU LOOK SO DIFFERENT!" I exclaimed first thing Thursday morning. Rachel was standing in the middle of C wing. Already a whole crowd of our friends had gathered around her. Everyone was ooing and aahing over her new 'do.

"You look so elegant. Like a model in a magazine," Liza told her.

"You seem older, too," Chloe said.

"It's a huge change. I can't believe you had the guts," Felicia added.

"Me, neither," Rachel said. "But I'm so glad I did. I love it!"

Everyone loved it. Rachel had followed the advice from the website, and framed her square-shaped face with long, soft bangs. Her hairdresser had taken about four inches off the bottom, so her hair now fell just below her shoulders. It was layered, too, so it seemed much thicker and fuller.

"What's going on here, a nerd convention?" Claire shouted out as she approached our crowd. She stopped and stared for a moment at Rachel. She opened her mouth as if to say something, but nothing came out. She just stood there, her eyes wide with surprise. A moment later, she walked away, without saying a word.

"Wow!" Felicia exclaimed. "You did it, Rach. You actually shut Claire up!"

"I think we should all go get new haircuts." I laughed.

"Not today," Chloe said. "Today's baby-sitting day."

"You guys are going to have so much fun," Liza remarked wistfully. "I wish I didn't have my tutor today."

"It's okay, you can come next time," Chloe told her. "We plan on turning this into a regular thing."

I shook my head. Once again, Chloe was being slightly over-ambitious. "Let's just get through today," I said.

Rachel, Chloe, and I hurried off the bus and ran to my house after school. We had to set up the backyard before all the little kids got there.

"It's really nice of your mom to let us use the backyard for this," Chloe said.

"She was so relieved when she heard it wasn't going to rain today. I think the idea of four little kids running around the house was too much for her to handle," I told Chloe, as I set up cups of beads and pieces of yellow lanyard on our picnic table. "This will be our craft table," I explained.

"I've got the sports center set up!" Felicia called. She pointed to a crack in the sidewalk where she'd placed a shiny penny. "We're going to play hit-the-penny," she added, holding up a pink rubber ball. "That's this game where two kids stand on either side of the penny, and try to hit it with the ball. It's one point for a hit, and two if you flip the penny over."

"That's such a fun game. I used to play with my cousins," Rachel said. She pulled a bag of hair ribbons, old shirts, and soft felt hats from her backpack and dumped them on the grass. "The dress-up area is ready," she announced.

"Wow! This is great!" Chloe exclaimed. "The kids are going to have so much fun."

"Hey," Felicia interrupted her. "If I'm doing sports, Jenny's doing crafts, and Rachel's got dress-up covered, what are *you* doing?"

"I'm going to help all of you guys," Chloe said. "The computer said I'm a natural with kids, so I want all of them to get a chance to be around me."

"Oh, brother." Felicia groaned, rolling her eyes.

"You know what I mean," Chloe told her. "I'll be the one who helps out if anything gets too crazy."

"Let's hope it doesn't," I said, remembering the dog disaster.

"It'll be okay," Chloe promised me. "Kids are much easier than dogs. You can talk to them and tell them what to do."

Just then, my mother walked out into the backyard. She was followed by two little boys.

"Jason and Michael are here," my mom announced. "Mrs. Thomas just dropped them off."

Chloe was the first to run over to the boys. "Hi there," she greeted them. "I'm Chloe."

Jason, who was five years old, stuck out his chubby hand. "I'm Jason," he said, trying to sound very grown-up.

Chloe shook his hand, and then pulled hers away quickly. "Sticky hand," she said.

"It's from my jelly sandwich," Jason told her.

"Didn't you wash your hands before you came?" Chloe asked him.

Jason shook his head. "I like to lick off the jelly," he told her, taking a big lick of his hand. Chloe made a face, but she didn't say anything.

Three-year-old Michael reached up and wiped his nose with his sleeve. "Gotta cold," he said.

"I'll get you some tissues," I said, hurrying toward the house.

"He doesn't need them," Jason told me. "He's just gonna use his shirt anyway."

I frowned. Little boys were pretty gross. I couldn't wait for the girls to arrive. I had a feeling they would be much cleaner.

A few minutes later, five-year-old Julia Wilensky showed up. She was wearing a pink tutu and white tights. She looked a lot sweeter than Michael or Jason.

"What a pretty ballerina you are," I told Julia.

"I'm a fairy princess," Julia said. She held up her sparkly, star-shaped wand.

"Oh, I'm so sorry, your highness," I apologized with a grin.

"It's okay," Julia told me. "I wear this when I want to be a ballerina sometimes, too."

"Who are we waiting for?" Rachel asked Chloe.

"Cecilia Katsalis. She should be here any minute," Chloe said. Then, turning to Julia she added, "You'll like Cecilia. She's very nice. And she's five years old, just like you."

A few moments later, a shy girl in blue jeans and a red T-shirt walked into the backyard. "You must be Cecilia," I said, walking over to greet her.

Cecilia looked up at me and started to cry. "I wanna go home," she sobbed. "I don't like it here."

Felicia raced over to her. She lived on the same block as Cecilia and had been the one to get her to come. We all hoped she could calm Cecilia down.

"We're gonna have a great time, Cecilia," she promised her. "Look at all the fun stuff there is to do."

"Can we have a water fight?" Cecilia asked. "I love water fights."

Felicia shook her head. "It's a little too chilly for that."

"Can we bake cookies, then?" Cecilia suggested.

I shook my head. "We're going to have tons of fun out here," I told her. "We can't use the kitchen."

"This is gonna stink," Cecilia groaned.

"No, it won't," Chloe told her. "We're going to have fun. Why don't you go make some nice bead necklaces with Jenny?" I raised my hand so she could see who I was.

"Don't wanna," Cecilia said.

"*I* wanna make a necklace," Michael said. "*Aachoo.*"

I tried not to look as Michael wiped his nose with his sleeve again. Then I walked over to the bead table with him and got him started stringing the plastic beads on some yellow cord.

"Do you want to play dress-up?" Rachel asked Cecilia.

"No."

"Oh, I do! I do!" Julia squealed. "Can we play beauty parlor?"

"That's one of my favorite games," Rachel said excitedly. "I have lots of hair bows you can try on. Come on. We can play together."

That just left Jason and Cecilia. "Let's go play hit-the-penny," Felicia urged, walking the two five-year-olds to the sidewalk. "Boy against girl."

"I'm gonna win," Jason announced.

"Oh, no, you're not!" Cecilia countered.

For a few minutes, everything seemed to be working out perfectly in the backyard. Then, suddenly, I heard fighting coming from the sidewalk. I turned to see what was happening.

"You cheated!" Cecilia shouted.

"Did not. I hit that penny and it flipped over," Jason yelled back.

"You were standing too close," Cecilia told him.

"Let's have a do-over," Felicia suggested.

"That's not fair!" Jason screamed.

"Is too!" Cecilia shouted back.

"Oh, yeah?" Jason growled, his eyes getting small and angry.

Suddenly, Cecilia lunged at Jason. He curled his small hands into fists. Felicia just managed to jump between them before they could hit each other.

Unfortunately for her, that was the exact moment that Cecilia tried to throw the ball really hard at Michael. Instead of hitting Michael, it got Felicia right in the eye.

"*Ouch!*" Felicia shouted, putting her hands to her face. "Now see what you two have done!"

"She did it," Jason said.

Cecilia didn't say anything.

"I'll go get some ice!" Chloe shouted, running for the house.

As I turned my attention back to Michael, I noticed he had a finger up his nose.

"How about I get you that tissue now?" I asked him.

"I'm not picking my nose," Michael explained. "I'm just trying to get the bead out."

"You stuck a bead in your nose?" I gulped.

Michael nodded. "Wanted to see if it fit. It did. Now I can't get it out!" He pulled his finger from his nose and screamed. "My nose is bleeding!" he shouted.

This was bad. *Real bad.* I grabbed Michael by his arm and pulled him toward the house. "Mom! Help!" I screamed as we ran in the door.

A little while later, everything had quieted down. Mom

had used her tweezers to get the bead from Michael's nose. Felicia had placed an ice pack over her eye. It was kind of purple, but not too bad. Chloe was quietly reading to Michael, Cecilia, and Jason. I'm not sure the two older kids really liked listening to a story instead of playing, but after all the trouble they'd caused, I think they were afraid to argue.

As I came out of the house with glasses of lemonade for everyone, I smiled to myself. The afternoon was almost over, and we hadn't lost anyone, or caused any serious damage.

By the time the kids' mothers had come by to pick them up, I was exhausted. I plopped down on the grass and took a deep breath.

"That wasn't so bad, was it?" Chloe said with a smile, sitting down next to me. "Should we do it again next week?"

I remembered Michael's bloody nose. Then I looked over at Felicia with her black-and-blue eye, and Rachel, who still sported the multiple pigtails Julia had given her while they were playing beauty parlor.

"I don't think so," I told Chloe.

"Why not?" Chloe asked. "I had fun with the kids."

"Yeah, that's because no one bled on you or hit you in the eye or knotted up your hair," I told her. "I officially retire from baby-sitting."

"Me, too," Rachel said, pulling a bow from her hair.

"That goes triple for me," Felicia added.

Chloe shrugged and looked down at the money in her

hand. "Well, I'm almost there. All I need is ten dollars more. Any of you guys have any other ideas about how I can earn some money?"

"No!" Rachel and Felicia shouted at once.

"Ouch!" I added, bumping my head on the picnic table as I reached over to pick up some of Michael's fallen beads.

I reached up and felt a small lump starting to form on my skull. That settled it. From now on, when it came to making money, Chloe was on her own. I was officially retired – at least until I was old enough to get a real job. One that didn't involve dogs or little kids!

Chapter EIGHT

I PRACTICALLY COLLAPSED into my chair as I reached our lunch table on Friday. It was only fifth period, but I was already completely wiped out.

"What's wrong?" Liza asked me.

"What *isn't*?" I groaned. "First, I had a really rough surprise quiz in English, and then, Mr. Conte made me do a math problem up at the board – which I got wrong, of course. As if that wasn't bad enough, I got a big, fat C on my history paper, which is not going to make my parents happy."

"Oh, wow," Liza said sympathetically. "Well, just relax. You're among friends now."

"Absolutely," Carolyn agreed.

"Friends forever," Marilyn seconded. "Oh, look, there are Chloe and Marc. Boy, they're late getting to lunch."

I waved in their direction. But only Chloe could see me. Marc's view of our table was blocked by the sudden appearance of a dark-haired eighth-grader named Cassidy. I knew who she was because she had the part of Lucy in *You're a Good Man, Charlie Brown.* Chloe was a little jealous of Cassidy. Lucy was the part she had auditioned for.

Suddenly, Cassidy thrust her arms out in front of her. "Romeo, Romeo, wherefore art thou, Romeo?" she said loudly.

Marc rolled his eyes and walked right past her. He hurried over to our table and plopped down his book bag. Chloe took the seat next to him and pulled out her bag lunch.

"What was that about?" I asked Marc.

"An audition," he replied.

"For what?" I asked him.

"My movie," Marc replied sadly.

"I thought it was a spontaneous documentary," Chloe reminded him. "At least that what's you told me."

"It is," Marc said. "Or at least it *was.* I'm not making my movie anymore."

"Why?" I asked him, surprised.

Marc reached into his backpack and yanked out the newest edition of the *Joyce Kilmer Gazette.* "Madame X," he declared angrily. "That's why!"

I hadn't had a chance to read the school paper yet – not with my lousy morning. So I took the paper from his hand and read this week's "In the Know with Madame X."

There's a director in our midst, folks! Just look for the seventh-grader with the video camera lurking in the halls. He's making a movie about us – so be careful. You don't want your darkest secrets to appear on film.

"Oh, but it's okay for everyone's darkest secrets to appear in a newspaper column?" Chloe asked sarcastically. "That's what Madame X is writing about. Whoever she is, she's a real hypocrite."

"Seriously," Marilyn said.

"Big time," Carolyn agreed.

"But why does this have to be the end of your movie?" I asked Marc. "Think of it as publicity."

"Yeah, *bad* publicity," Marc groaned. "Now I can't get anyone to be natural around me," he said. "They either avoid me or audition for me. I can't make a realistic documentary that way."

"I'm not the only one who's going to be angry," Marc continued. "Just wait until Josh sees this."

"I think he already has," Chloe said. "Look."

She pointed over to the cafeteria food line. Josh was practically hiding behind his books. And he was wearing dark sunglasses.

"I think he's traveling incognito," Marilyn giggled.

"You would be, too, if you read what Madame X wrote," Marc said.

I looked down at the page. *What blond-haired, green-eyed, eighth-grade bookworm has a crush on the librarian, Miss Hopkins?* "That can't be Josh," I said.

"Not that one. Keep going," Marc said.

Which Pop girl made up an imaginary boyfriend from another school, and even went so far as to send herself text messages to make it more believable?

"Oh, that's gotta be Elena," Marilyn said. "Didn't she give herself a valentine in third grade?"

"I think that was Maya," Carolyn countered.

"It could be Dana," Chloe suggested. "She's just weird enough to try that."

"Well, no matter who it is, it's not Josh," I pointed out.

"Check out the last paragraph," Marc told me, pointing to the part he meant.

I read on.

He's a math nerd, she's a jock. This time it's the girl who is going to wind up scoring points for the school. Makes you wonder just who wears the pants in this geek un-chic relationship.

"Ouch," Liza said. "That's really not nice. It makes Josh sound like a wimpy weakling instead of a black belt."

"Why didn't Madame X mention his tae kwon do?" Marilyn wondered out loud. "He's really good at that."

"She never writes anything *good* about anyone," Carolyn reminded her sister.

"Where's Josh going?" Liza asked as she watched him head over toward the door.

"Probably to eat lunch on the stairs," Marc said. "My guess is he's too embarrassed to eat in public."

"Yeah, well, Josh will be okay. And your movie will be,

too," I told Marc. "This will blow over by next week – as soon as there's a new Madame X column."

"I don't know about that," Marc said. "The Pops are still mad at each other."

I looked around the room. Marc was right. Addie and her friends – or former friends – were still scattered around the cafeteria.

"What I don't get is how Madame X finds out her information," Marc continued. "I mean, nobody knew what my movie was about except for you guys. And none of you would tell . . ." He stopped for a minute and looked at us accusingly. "Or would you?"

"Come on, Marc. You know we would never . . ." Chloe began.

"Do I?" Marc demanded. "You were pretty mad when I wouldn't let you sing in the film, Chloe."

"Oh, give me a break," Chloe replied. "Why would I tell Madame X anything after she spread a rumor about me?"

"Okay, maybe it wasn't you. Maybe it was someone else." He glanced at Liza, the twins, and me. "Madame X hasn't mentioned any of you four," he said suspiciously. "It could be one of you."

"Me?" Liza asked him, unable to mask her shock. "I would never do anything like that."

"Me, neither!" Marilyn and Carolyn said at the same time.

"Marc, we're all friends," I assured him. "None of us would ever do anything to hurt you – or Josh and Felicia."

"Well, somebody must have told her, then," Marc said, grabbing his stuff and standing up.

"Where are you going?" Liza asked him.

"To sit by myself," Marc growled. "I don't want any more information about me leaked into the school paper."

"Oh, chill out," Chloe told him. "We're not going to reveal your deep, dark secrets. None of us even know who Madame X is."

I sighed heavily. I sure hoped we would find out soon. Maybe then we could convince her to stop.

"I just don't understand Madame X," Felicia cried to me on the bus that afternoon. "Why is she so mean? What kind of person would do this?"

"I don't know," I told her.

"And where does she get her information from?" Felicia continued. "I mean, it's like she's a fly on the wall when people are having private conversations. She hears everything! How can no one know who she is?"

"It is really weird," I agreed. "Like someone is spying on us all the time."

"It gives me the creeps," Felicia said. "I feel like I can't trust anyone. Not even my closest friends."

"That's ridiculous," I told her. "You can trust your real friends."

"Really?" Felicia asked me. "That's not how you felt a couple days ago. You thought I had told Madame X about Chloe having a secret, remember?"

I blushed. She had me there. "Yeah. But you didn't and I was wrong," I said apologetically. "I know you would never reveal a secret like that. None of us would ever be that mean to anyone."

Felicia shrugged. "I guess not," she said. But I could tell she wasn't completely convinced.

To tell you the truth, I wasn't, either.

Chapter NINE

"THAT WAS SO MUCH FUN!" Felicia squealed as we rode the bus to school together on Monday.

"I know," I agreed. "It was so amazing that your mother let us go into the store all by ourselves while she waited in the food court."

"Well, we *are* in middle school now," Felicia said.

"And I can't believe we got to see Chloe try on a dress! I've never seen her in anything but shorts and jeans," I exclaimed. "I am so glad her parents gave her the rest of the money she needed."

"We are going to be the hottest people at the dance next weekend!" Felicia proclaimed.

Speaking of which . . . I glanced behind me to where Addie was sitting. She was all by herself, staring out the window. No cell phone conversations for her today.

The Pops must still be fighting over Madame X's column. Which meant that they hadn't been together this weekend. They all were probably just sitting at home doing nothing . . . alone. The era of world domination by the Pops had ended.

Or not. As soon as I walked over to my locker in C wing,

I saw Claire, Dana, and Elena enter the school together. They were walking in the direction of Addie's locker. And they seemed perfectly happy.

So much for my theory.

I stood there for a minute, waiting for one of them to make some snide comment about my old sneakers or Felicia's braids, but they walked right past us.

And then the strangest thing happened.

The Pops turned on Addie.

"Traitor," Claire hissed.

"Snitch," Dana growled loud enough for everyone to hear.

"Freak," Elena said, adding the cruelest cut of all.

Addie looked as though she was going to cry. But she didn't. She just looked in the mirror and smeared more pink gloss on her lips.

"Okay, so what was that all about?" Felicia asked me curiously.

"Don't ask me," I replied. "But I'll bet you anything it has something to do with Madame X."

For the first time since school began, I actually had a good time in gym class that day. With Dana and Addie not whispering to each other and laughing at everyone else, I was able to relax and really get into the volleyball game we were playing.

"Nice serve," Addie congratulated me, after one of my particularly good whacks over the net.

I looked to see if she was kidding. But she wasn't. It was a real compliment.

But I wasn't going to fall for that again. Last time Addie had been nice to me I'd almost fallen for it. I'd sat there in that student government office and talked to her all about how great Felicia was doing, and how exciting Marc's movie was. . . .

And then it hit me. *Wham!*

Addie hadn't just been nice to me because the Pops were fighting. She'd been pumping me for information.

Information she could use in her newspaper column.

Because Addie was Madame X.

It all made sense. Only a Pops insider would have known about Claire sucking her thumb, or about one of the Pops sending herself a valentine. As for that column she wrote about Chloe, well, she'd probably heard Felicia and me talking about it on the school bus. Now which one of us was eavesdropping?

Apparently the Pops had figured out Madame X's identity, too. It couldn't have been too tough. After all, while all of their deep dark secrets were in the school paper, there had never been any rumors about Addie. Which must have led them to conclude that she was Madame X. That explained why none of the Pops were talking to Addie.

MIDDLE SCHOOL RULE # 15:

KEEP YOUR FRIENDS' SECRETS. OTHERWISE YOU WON'T HAVE ANY FRIENDS!

"So, are we going to work on the finishing touches for the dance today after school?" Addie asked me hopefully as our volleyball team rotated positions.

The last thing I wanted to do was spend the afternoon working side by side with the notorious Madame X. "I think you've got it under control," I told her.

"You're not going to make me do this whole thing alone, are you?" Addie asked me. "I thought we were supposed to be working on the Luau together."

Funny, that's not how she'd been acting a few days ago. When we'd first started planning the dance, she'd tried her best to leave me out of everything. But ever since her friends dumped her . . .

I had to stop myself from thinking like that. After all, I was still class president. And no matter how I felt about Addie right now, I had responsibilities.

"Sure, fine. I'll meet you after school at the student council office," I said as the other team's server sent the ball flying over the net. I reached up and hit the volleyball really, really hard.

"Oh, good, you're here," Addie said, looking up cheerfully as I came into the student council office after my last class. She tried to smile, but I could tell she'd been crying. Her eyes were all red, and her cheeks were kind of damp.

"Something wrong?" I asked her as nicely as I could. I was really, really mad at Addie, but I just can't be mean to someone who's crying.

"N-n-no," Addie said, stumbling over the word. "I mean, not really."

I took a deep breath before I said anything else. I wasn't really sure how Addie was going to react to this. Finally I told her, "You knew they would figure it out sooner or later, Addie."

She looked at me with surprise. "I don't know what you're talking about."

"Oh, come on," I said, getting braver by the minute. "If *I* was able to figure out Madame X's secret identity, I know your friends could."

"Madame X?" Addie asked in a voice that sounded kind of fake. "You mean that gossip columnist in the school paper?"

"I mean *you*," I said flatly. "I know it was you who printed all that stuff about my friends. I know because you got all that information from me. I mean you've done some pretty mean stuff to me this year, Addie, but being nice to me just so you could find out secrets about my friends is the worst. And you twisted all my words around and made everything sound horrible."

Addie sighed heavily. There was no way she was

getting out of this, and she knew it. "Look, I *had* to write that stuff," she told me finally. "My friends were all fighting with each other about the column I'd written before that one. I figured if I wrote a lot of junk about *your* friends, then . . ."

"Then they'd start making fun of Marc or Felicia and Josh, and forget they were fighting with each other," I said, finishing her thought.

Addie nodded. "And it worked, sort of," she said. "Except now *they're* all friends, but they hate me."

"Can you blame them?" I asked her honestly. "You published all their most personal secrets in the school newspaper."

"I was just having fun," Addie insisted. "It was all a joke. No one's feelings were supposed to get hurt. That's why I didn't use any names."

"We all figured it out, though," I reminded her.

"I know," Addie admitted sadly. "And by now, Claire and Dana have told the whole school it was me who wrote the columns. *Everyone* is going to hate me!"

I stared at the piles of decorations all around the office. I thought about all the money we'd already spent on the food we'd ordered. If Addie didn't do something soon to fix this mess, it would all go to waste.

"Look, Addie, you're going to have to apologize for what you did," I told her. "Because if you don't, everyone will be too mad at you to come to the luau."

"Oh, people wouldn't do that," Addie said. "It's going to

be a great time. People will come just to dance, to hear a real band, and eat pizza."

"Most people were coming to the party because *you* planned it, Addie," I told her honestly. "Kids around here look up to you." I hated saying it, but I knew it was true. "But they won't respect you unless you come clean about all this. Just admit you made a mistake. Your friends will forgive you if you do that."

Addie started to cry again. "Do you really think so?" she whimpered.

I nodded. "I'm sure of it," I said, even though I really wasn't. There was no way to predict how the Pops would react to anything. "And once they forgive you, everyone else will, too."

I sure hoped I was right. Otherwise we were going to have one lousy luau on Friday.

That night, I sat in front of my computer, staring at a blank screen. I knew I was supposed to be doing my English homework. I was supposed to be doing thirty minutes of free writing but all I could think about was the luau. I was really worried that it was going to be a disaster. What if Addie was too chicken to admit what she had done? What if she blamed it all on someone else and only made things worse?

I had to get my mind off that party! Otherwise I'd never be able to do my homework. There had to be a way to distract myself from all this pressure.

Then, my fingers started to move as though they had a mind of their own. Only they weren't typing a paragraph. They were taking me to my favorite website. Which wasn't a bad idea, actually. If I couldn't concentrate enough to write, at least I could entertain myself with a quick quiz.

Hey, Cookie!

Everyone knows you're sweet as sugar. But does your sugary soul come with some spice? To find out what cookie you're most like, take this tasty quiz.

1. **You promised your mom you'd go shopping with her after school, but the guy you've been crushin' on just asked you to go to the mall with him instead. What do you do?**

   A. Explain that you have to do something with your mom, but you'd really like to hang with him tomorrow.
   B. Pretend you forgot about your date with your mom, and ditch her.
   C. Get your mom to give you money and promise to buy whatever she needs while you're hanging with your new fave guy.

That one was easy. I don't break plans with people. I wouldn't want them to do that to me. (Not that my mom ever would!) I clicked on A.

2. **If you could have the perfect school schedule, which class would be first thing every morning?**

   A. Study hall — I'm not a morning person!

B. Math. I like to jump right into the hard stuff.
C. Gym class. Gotta get up and get movin'!

Definitely A. Getting up in the morning in time to make the bus is the thing I hate most in life.

3. It's school assembly time. Everyone's piling into the auditorium. Where can you usually be found?

A. Snoozing in your seat.
B. Giggling in the back with your gal pals.
C. Sitting in the front row, trying to pay attention. After all, you don't want to insult the speakers.

Before I ran for class president, I probably would have been one of the gigglers from letter B. But ever since I'd had to give my speech for the class president elections, I knew how hard it was to get up in front of a bunch of kids and speak. I clicked C.

4. That huge school project is due tomorrow! What's your plan?

A. All done. I never save stuff for the last minute.
B. *Achoo*. Think I've got the flu. I'm gonna have to miss school for a day or two ☺
C. It's time to pull an all-nighter!

My answer to that one was definitely A. But not because I like working weeks ahead of time on projects. It's just that if I don't start my work early, my dad will nag me until I do. In the long run, it's easier to just get it done.

Add Up Your Score

1. A. 1 point B. 3 points C. 2 points
2. A. 2 points B. 1 point C. 3 points
3. A. 2 points B. 3 points C. 1 point
4. A. 1 point B. 3 points C. 2 points

What's the recipe behind your personality?

4-6 points: Sugar Cookie

You're always reliable, and always delicious. That makes you special because your friends know you'll always be there for them. And just like a sugar cookie is consistent throughout, your pals can rest assured that you'll never go bitter or nutty on them when they least expect it.

7-10 points: Cream-Filled Sandwich Cookie

Everybody loves you, but for different reasons. Just like some people eat the cream first, while others prefer to shove the whole cookie in their mouths, you seem to have a little something for everyone. And like this super-stuffed cookie, you are always able to hold yourself together, even in tough situations.

11-12 points: Chocolate Chocolate Chunk Cookie with Marshmallows and Nuts

You're the wild child of the cookie aisle. Your friends never know what they're gonna get. With each bite there's a new surprise. The only constant in your life is that it's all delicious and crazy. But you might want to take a deep breath and slow down a bit. A cookie this rich could get to be too much.

With a five-point score, I was a sweet, dependable sugar cookie. That was a nice thought. But even better, I'd found a theme for my free writing essay. Quickly, I typed in my title: *Kids are Like Desserts.*

One problem solved.

The next morning, I discovered that Addie had solved my other problem as well. She'd written her apology, printed it out on paper, and distributed it to as many kids as possible.

In the Know with Madame X

Usually this column has a no-names policy. But today I'm changing that. I'm going to identify myself. I am Addie Wilson and I am really sorry I ever started writing this column. I guess I didn't realize that people would be so hurt by the things I wrote. The secrets I wrote about didn't seem so important. But, I realize now that secrets are secrets for a reason. So I apologize to all of my friends if I hurt them in any way. And I hope to see all of you at the luau on Friday.

I stood there in the middle of C wing and stared at the newspaper in my hand. I hadn't expected Addie to be this honest about what she had done.

"Pretty impressive," I said, walking over to Addie's locker.

Dana and Claire came up behind me. "She wasn't apologizing to you, freak," Dana grumbled. "Read it carefully. She apologized to her *friends*. That definitely doesn't include you."

"That's for sure," Claire agreed. She turned to Addie. "Got any more of that light brown eyeshadow?" she asked her. "I'm all out."

"Sure," Addie said, a big smile forming on her face. "Here you go."

I stood there for a minute, waiting to see if Addie would thank me for my advice. But she didn't. In fact, she basically ignored me.

Which meant everything was completely back to normal.

Chapter TEN

"ALOHA!" I SAID, placing a floral lei around Rachel's neck as she entered the school cafeteria. I'd been doing it to everyone as they arrived at the luau.

"Whoa! Check this place out," Rachel said, looking around the cafeteria. "You guys did an awesome job."

"It was mostly Addie," I admitted. "But I *am* the one who ordered the cakes shaped like volcanoes." I pointed over to one of the snack tables, where several cone-shaped cakes with red icing dripping all over them were placed.

"Mmm, yummy," Rachel said. "Hey, do you know what one volcano said to the other?"

"What?"

"I lava you!" She laughed.

"I lava you, too," I said with a giggle. "I lava all of my friends."

"Speaking of which, have you seen Felicia?" Rachel asked.

"She's dancing with Josh," I said, pointing toward the dance floor. "Liza and Chloe are getting flowers painted on their faces, and Marc is over by the food. I'm not sure where the twins are."

"I like the purple flower on your cheek," Rachel complimented me.

"It's supposed to be an orchid," I told her.

"It's really pretty. And it matches the purple flowers in your skirt. Do you think Liza would paint a flower on my face?"

"Of course! Go ask her."

As Rachel wandered off toward the girls' room, I stepped back and took a look at how the luau was going. So far, so good. Lots of people were dancing. Addie had been right. A live, high school band was really cool – even if they only knew six songs.

As the band finished playing, Ms. Gold, our principal, hopped up on the stage. "Boys and girls," she said into the microphone. "May I have your attention, please?"

She tapped the microphone twice with her finger, but the kids in the room kept laughing, talking, and running around.

Suddenly a burst of feedback shot out of the guitarist's amplifier. Now *that* got everyone's attention!

Ms. Gold laughed as everyone suddenly turned to the stage. Even she was in a good mood tonight.

"I hope you're all having a great time!" Ms..Gold shouted into the microphone.

"Oh, yeah!" the kids all shouted back at once.

"We have two special people to thank for tonight," Ms. Gold continued. "Will Addie Wilson and Jenny McAfee come up on stage for a minute?"

I blushed beet red. I didn't want to go up on that stage in front of all those people. That wasn't my thing. I'm more of a behind-the-scenes person.

Addie, on the other hand, couldn't get up there fast enough. She raced up the stairs and took her place in the spotlight. I followed behind her, blushing all the way.

And there we were, Addie Wilson and Jenny McAfee, together again. Of course, it wasn't the same as it had once been. But as I looked out at my cheering friends, I realized that that was okay. Change could be good. I had my friends and Addie had hers. And as long as we didn't have to spend *too* much time together, we could pretty much coexist.

"Okay, everybody, let's limbo!" the lead singer of the band shouted into his microphone. Ms. Gold leaped down from the stage and took one end of the limbo pole. Mr. Schwartz, one of the art teachers, grabbed the other end. And then the music started.

"How low can you go? How low can you go?" the singer began to chant.

As I hopped into line beside Rachel and Chloe, I noticed that Addie and her friends weren't joining us.

"Guess this isn't a Pops thing," I said.

"They think it's beneath them," Rachel joked. "Get it, under the limbo pole? *Beneath . . .*"

"I get it," I said with a laugh. But I didn't really. I mean, I understood the *joke*. What I didn't understand was why the Pops always thought it was uncool to have fun.

Not me. I could sink pretty low, if it meant having a good time. And to prove it, I bent over backwards and slid my way under the limbo bar.

"Go, Jenny!" Marc cheered me on, as he filmed the limbo contest. Obviously, he wasn't letting Madame X get in the way of his making his movie anymore.

I looked around the room. My friends were all laughing, smiling, and having a great time. So was I. This was the perfect night: amazing friends, yummy food, and lots of fun. I was the happiest I'd ever been in my whole life.

I opened my mouth wide and let out a loud yell. "Middle school rocks!" I shouted. And I meant it!

Are You Too Cool for School?

Take this computer quiz and find out how you score on the diva meter!

1. **How do you react when a friend is fifteen minutes late meeting you at the movies?**

   A. You're kind of annoyed, but you'll get over it as soon as you get your popcorn.
   B. No big deal. It was fun to people watch in the lobby as you waited.
   C. You get your ticket and go in without her. You're not going to have a lousy seat just because she's late!

2. **What kind of animal are you most like?**

   A. A fun-loving puppy who always wants to go out for a walk.
   B. A sweet and simple goldfish, happily swimming around in her bowl.
   C. A finicky kitty with a passion for caviar.

3. **Your family is planning a vacation and your brother suggests camping. What's your first reaction?**

   A. You'll go along with it — as long as you get to stop at a water park along the way. You love those log flume rides!
   B. Sleeping under the stars sounds like so much fun. First dibs on the marshmallows!
   C. Unless camping means a hotel with cable TV, you're not going!

4. **How long does it take you to get ready to go to a school dance?**

   A. About two hours — you've got to iron your new skirt, wash and dry your hair, put on a little blush, lip gloss, and eye shadow, and find a cute pair of shoes in your closet for dancing.

   B. You can be ready in five minutes. A clean pair of jeans, a cute shirt, a little lip gloss, and you're good to go.

   C. Two weeks, minimum. That's how long it will take you to buy a new outfit, make an appointment to get your hair cut, and invite the girls over to give each other manicures.

The Diva Meter

So how much of a pampered princess are you?

Mostly A's: Although you like the finer things in life, you're not opposed to a little low-maintenance fun. You've managed to strike a great balance in your life!

Mostly B's: There's not an ounce of diva blood flowing through your veins. But maybe you should consider thinking about yourself a little every once in a while. You deserve it!

Mostly C's: Girl, you put the D in diva. That's D for demanding. Tone it down a bit, and give in from time to time — you might get more back than you expect!

NANCY KRULIK HAS WRITTEN more than 150 books for children and young adults, including three *New York Times* bestsellers. She is the author of the popular Katie Kazoo Switcheroo series and is also well known as a biographer of Hollywood's hottest young stars. Her knowledge of the details of celebrities' lives has made her a desired guest on several entertainment shows on the E! network as well as on *Extra* and *Access Hollywood.* Nancy lives in Manhattan with her husband, composer Daniel Burwasser, their two children, Ian and Amanda, and a crazy cocker spaniel named Pepper.